SMOKE JUMPERS

SMOKE JUMPERS

by

NELS JORGENSEN

THE CHILDREN'S PRESS
LONDON AND GLASGOW

To
ALBERT T. ERLER

CONTENTS

CHAPTER ONE

IN TRAINING

THE big wide-winged monoplane swerved sharply, then banked on one wing to come in low over the wasted ground. From the clouds the long miles of smoke-blackened forest looked as though a painter had forgotten himself and gone splashing crazy white and grey streaks at random. As far as the horizon to the northward the forest of living trees stuck up helplessly out of billowing black clouds of smoke, only the tops of them to be seen where the smoke rolled back in places, with the shifting currents of air.

Now and then the updraft from the pockets where fire had burned out oxygen caused the big plane to stagger, then right itself.

From the air it was a wild scene. One or two of the men behind Rick Harding in the plane's cabin had seen forest fires before, but none of them had ever been quite this close to one. Now Rick knew what he had been trained for!

This was his enemy—fire!

And he was a fire fighter, a " smoke jumper."

One of Uncle Sam's tested young men, trained and equipped to fight the menace of forest fires in every part of the United

States and its territories. Mostly the smoke jumpers were very young, for it took youth to become and to stay hard enough for the hazardous work.

Rick Harding might have looked a little older than his nineteen years as he stood there, swaying with the plane's slight motion and staring out of the bay, his grey eyes narrowed. He had to shift a little when the floor under him tipped.

His lean young body was hard and fit and his darkly sunburned face was cool and open. His eyes showed the inner knowledge of what he had been trained to do, would be doing daily after the ceremonies of graduation soon to come.

Fight fire—fight it in Uncle Sam's millions of acres of precious forest preserves, from Maine to Oregon, from the Mexican Border to the Canadian line—where the Canadian Government took up its own task of checking this terrible menace on its own vast preserves.

It had been drilled into the cadets that

the work to come would be largely with the Canadian rangers ; there was a co-operative spirit existing between the two.

A voice just behind him came to Rick's ears above the roar of the big motors. " They won't be sending us down to-day, after all—we haven't officially graduated yet. They just wanted us to get a good look at what it means, I guess. Boy, a jump down into that would be something, heh?—even with all our equipment! "

Rick nodded, his eyes returning to the scene below. His companion, one of seven trainees about to be graduated from the Government Base for forest fire fighters, stared too. Young Ladd Malcolm was Rick's own age, blue-eyed and fearless-looking, toughened and hardened ; yet he too was feeling the danger and the great responsibility of their job.

" When they shifted our schools I didn't argue," Rick said. " But this part of the country is where I was raised." He pointed down past the bay. " It's lumber land, fine lumber—Douglas pine, mostly, and spruce and fir and cedar. Some of it's Government leased out ; some of it's privately owned. Man, I can't help thinking what loot this would be for the gods of the destroying fire world! "

His eyes shone. Rick felt that he had been born for this work. Often in his training he had encountered fear, and the training had been hard—it was still hard—but all his young life he had sworn to be what he was now, or what he was about to become—a "smoke jumper" in the United States Forestry Patrol!

The interior of the big transport plane held all the squad's equipment. There were racks where the big fireproof boots were ; the strange-looking things like football helmets that each smoke jumper wore when he took his jump, protection for his eyes and face ; the heavy gloves he put on ; the tanks of extinguisher fluid he strapped to his back, filled with chemical that could stream across any blaze and kill it.

Ladd Malcolm pressed against Rick's shoulder as they peered down.

Below lay the open, beautiful lands of the great Pacific north-west. For a year, since he had passed eighteen, Rick had been attending a Government School in the Carolinas. He had passed the examinations, but the training for forestry work is hard and complete. When he had said he wanted to train for "smoke-jumping" work, he had had to undergo a harder, more strenuous course.

The last course was a test of nerve and of a student's ability to act on his own.

For there was no one alongside you when your 'chute dropped you off down below there and you released it to enter the blazing arena of smoke and fire. If there *was* some-one, you couldn't see him! He'd landed maybe a half-mile or a mile away, depending on the wind drift.

Rick watched the curls of smoke, the massive clouds of it. He watched the tree-tops showing through them, his mouth tight. The smoke was turning black and thick, and it was rolling in great clouds, like —not like mushrooms, but like the black underpart of a toadstool deadly and poisonous.

There came the gleam of a small lake. Then it was blotted out by a great belching bulk of cloud that was like a giant's pillow being disturbed and pushed over on its side.

The plane winged over and the smoke-jumper cadets had the chance to observe the vast range of ruin that this present blaze had already caused. They said it was being brought under control at last—after raging for more than a week and costing millions of dollars in damage to timber. And human and animal lives as well.

This batch of cadets from the Government Forestry school was due for graduation a little ahead of time because of the urgent need for trained "smoke jumpers."

The "smoke-jumper" section of the Service was fairly new. Only recently had it been perfected separately from the rest. Before the use of men trained to spill out of the skies and fight flame on its own ground, Forestry men had had to be rushed by train and truck, or any means available, to the threatened spot. And often they arrived so late that most of the damage had been done before they got there.

The "smoke jumpers," while not equipped by themselves to handle a giant fire—which required wide reserves—were able to get to their jobs at the first report of any outbreak, and check what was possible until reserves could come up.

For this the training had to be arduous. Some of the smoke jumpers were trained to leap from helicopters, but most of them from Forestry Service Patrol planes. The training, intense as it was, cut down on the length of probation for Forestry Service recruits, which was normally two years.

"You ready," Ladd Malcolm smiled, "for your practice jumps and diploma?"

"As ready as I ever will be," Rick smiled

back. " In fact "—his eyes narrowing as he
surveyed the destruction over which the
roaring motors were carrying them—" I
wish they'd pass the word for a ' bail-out '
right now. Can't see much of what's below
for all that smoke down there, but I've got
it on you : I know what it looks like on
that ground anyway—I was raised hereabouts."

Rick thought back to his boyhood. To
his father—a Forest Ranger right in this
territory below. Until disgrace had clouded
his name and he had disappeared.

As he thought of this dark spot in his
younger years a cloud passed over Rick's
face. " Another story," he would have told
his friend Ladd Malcolm. And it was.

Rick's father had been a respected Forest
Ranger, a Senior Ranger ; that was before
the days of the "smoke jumpers" and the
helicopters and the big planes and all the
newer and more modern methods of combating forest fires.

His father was "missing." Believed either dead or else a man who had betrayed his trust, according to one's viewpoint. No one knew. Many had made guesses.

But the blot remained on the name.

Maybe even someone here, one of his fellow-rangers, knew of it. Rick had suspected more than once that Brad Hovey did. Hovey had as much as said once or twice that he knew something of it all. But it didn't matter.

Back there in the dead days of the last war, all the world—all of it except for one or two freedom-loving nations—had seemed to be in arms against a democratic spirit that at the last moment had risen against aggression, to fight out the most cruel war in history.

Rick's father, a veteran of one war, had been compelled to stay at his post here in the north-west. For one thing, the enemy threatened a landing. Government servants were needed at their posts. The Forestry Service of the Department of Agriculture asked its personnel to aid in what might be a threat to the West Coast; they worked with the Coast Guard, the Immigration Department, and the Army.

Resenting that he could not return to active service, the elder Harding proved himself more than once in his responsible position as Chief of the Forestry Service in that area. He had been looked up to, respected.

The men who had been left behind, most of them because the Government believed their duties lay here at home rather than with the overseas armies, had met one night and Harding had presented them with an idea. It was this:

A great many men in all the armies of freedom were already in the hands of the enemy. Prisoners. There were ways to aid these men. Women and children too. They must be suffering untold hardships.

Money was necessary; gold and silver mostly. This could be used to bribe guards at the prison camps. But it could also be used to aid prisoners to escape, provided a route and plans were ready for them.

It would take a lot of money, this plan Rick's father had formulated. A "Fund." But the elder Harding had been through a war, and though he had never been a prisoner, he knew what prisoners suffered.

Bribes cost gold, so did organisation. A lot of money had to be raised.

But those who listened to the plan found much in it. Rick Harding's father was made treasurer of the Fund.

Somehow, outsiders heard of it and subscriptions poured in, some even from abroad. The Fund was to be used for prisoners of all countries in prison camps—not only to help them to escape, but to aid them while they were still imprisoned, furnishing them with food, tobacco, and the needs of life. Which they were certainly not getting.

It was a patriotic move and it met with a great response. Money came flooding in.

Most of it was under cover. A lot of patriotic men and women did not want their interest to become known. But the Fund reached a great figure—it was rumoured there were even diamonds and pearls and other jewellery in it, sent on by mothers and sisters and loved ones of men overseas. And Rick's father, as treasurer of the Fund, was placed in charge of all the donations.

Then something happened. Harding had complained of being followed, of strange figures at the edge of the clearing where his line camp stood.

Without a word to anyone, except that he had this fear and the fear was known to be connected with the treasure he had been entrusted with, he went out one night—and the world had never seen him since. He simply vanished.

And with him vanished the treasure.

Enemies spoke up. They said that Harding had disappeared with the Fund and later that he had been seen in San Francisco. Rumours came and went with the years.

But Harding had never been seen again and the great treasure was lost.

That was all Rick knew. That, and the fact that many men believed his father had stolen the Fund and run off with it. The rumour became a legend. It had hung over the son of the Ranger in his boyhood, and it hung over him now.

A few had believed in Harding. One of these men was "Piney" Lane, the scarred old woodsman who was at the moment caretaker and chief guard of the Government grant in this very section unfolding below them.

But Harding's friends could prove no more than his enemies could prove, and so the ancient story dragged on. . .

Rick Harding found his stare brooding out past the bay, his eyes on the country he had known in his boyhood.

Maybe—maybe Fate had willed him to be sent back here, to uncover his father's story and clear his name! But that seemed impossible, after all these years, and even he was aware of it. But, he thought, there must have been some pattern in the route he had followed, the route that was bringing him, Rick Harding, "smoke jumper," back to where he had started.

CHAPTER TWO

MYSTERY AND TREASURE

HE nodded to Malcolm, whom he liked, and found the regard of a fellow-jumper whom he didn't like fixed on him, it seemed meaningly. He shrugged. Then he turned away and fumbled with the buckles of his parachute harness ; he wouldn't be needing it any more to-day. But he was aware, across the rounded belly of the big plane, of Brad Hovey's eyes following him, amused and knowing.

He didn't want to dislike Brad Hovey. Hovey was one of the last recruits to the course ; having been sent on from the school at Cornell University. A slim, dark youth, good-looking in a way, but with that always-mocking knowingness lying behind his blue eyes.

He and Hovey hadn't clicked from the start. Rick had always had the feeling that Hovey was secretly jeering at him.

But Hovey had never said anything ; he'd just looked, and smiled, as though he had guessed a secret. Maybe he had!

A lot of people guessed. That was the way when there were legends and rumours.

It had been the same at the last school . . . The smoke-jumpers' initial training base was located at Biltmore, North Carolina ; it had been there for over fifty years, the earliest school to be acknowledged by the Forestry Service.

It had been opened by Dr. C. A. Schenck in 1897, in connection with the doctor's work on the Vanderbilt estates. A year or so afterward it had been officially recognised. It had not been until 1900 that the Yale School of Forestry had opened, and, even now, the Yale School made no specialisation in the particular brand of training that had attracted Rick Harding.

Rick had had almost no money; he'd been brought up catch-as-catch-can among his father's friends—mostly Piney Lane, having jobs here and there. When he finished high school he had come more directly under Piney's wing. Piney was his father's closest friend and at the moment he was caretaker and guardian of a great acreage of Government land outside Pinnacle, close to the Canadian Border. The plane was heading towards there now.

A long, arduous road to get to where he was at the moment. Rick thought back:

The nerve-shattering days of training, the jumps, real ones, not practice, from the tops of towers. Stepping off into empty air, toes instinctively feeling out for friendly surfaces and knowing there were none there . . . waiting after you jerked the rip cord of your 'chute and held your breath until, first, the small handkerchief caught, then slowed you up; afterward, those agonised seconds until the big white expanse came unpackaged to give your armpits a hard jerk as the wind came under it—and then you were there, swaying in the air, guiding your course as best you might by steering tugs at the guy ropes on your harness. . . Yes, a long road to be sure.

It was always a grim thought, too, that no parachute, no matter how much it cost, could be guaranteed.

But it got you there! It took a big hole out of your stomach as you swayed over what you hoped was your landing spot, watching the trees and danger patches below you. It held and you were down, sometimes in a tree. Sometimes on water, depending on the wind and your own skill with the 'chute ropes, and—yes, on your luck.

Dropping supplies ... You had to learn that too, for sometimes crews were hemmed in by flame and even a smoke jumper couldn't get to them—or if he could it would have served no purpose. But they were always there.

Rick stopped his thinking. They were coming in now. His instinct told him even before his eyes confirmed it, with the slant of the floor forward and the consequent vacuum in his breathing. He went to the port and peered out. Ahead, rushing towards the big plane, lay the scattered buildings and the silver of the landing strip of the school. It was all over now bar the shouting. Final tests, then assignments.

He told himself that he hoped, when he got his assignment, he and Brad Hovey would not be in the same crew.

Odd, how he and Hovey had just not got along from the start! Actually he couldn't think of anything he actively disliked about Hovey—well, maybe one thing : that air Hovey had of knowing something and keeping it back. If he had any private knowledge, Rick wished he would come out with it.

But it hadn't come out yet. Surely the school knew of the story, even though there had never been anything "official." Old Piney Lane had denounced lying tongues and gossip-mongers when he had fought so hard for Rick's appointment in the Government school. Piney was partly crippled from his logging days and he had a bad limp, but he was still a fire-eater.

Rick's legs felt cramped as he piled out of the belly of the big plane, his harness unbuckled and slung over his shoulder. He found Malcolm alongside him.

Malcolm started to say something about Hovey, but broke off as a whistle blew at the edge of the tarmac.

The P.A. blared out across the field :

"All cadets up for graduation will appear

immediately after stowing gear, in the Assembly Hall. All cadets will appear imme . . ." The notice repeated itself.

Rick had been thinking of a shower. Here in the heart of the Pacific north-west forests it could get very warm in late spring. It had been hot down in the south too.

He missed the shower. He changed into a clean uniform, eyeing the crease in the long grey-green trousers that were for dress purposes only, and smiling to himself as he listened to the chatter. They were all talking about one thing :

"Assignments! "

For they all assumed they were to be graduated.

That was a fair enough thing to take for granted. The long course of training had eliminated a few of them before now. Rick could think back on names he had known, faces, from months back—gone now. Gently but firmly the seeding process had been undertaken. A student wasn't called a quitter or a coward or even less than a man just because he was not found fit for this hard job. To some the rigours of training were irksome.

Training for "smoke jumping" was not just the ability to take parachute jumps and know what to do when one landed in a fire area. It covered much more than that.

The colonel in charge of the school—Colonel Moore had only recently been appointed—summed it up, when they were all there in front of him, a quiet, respectful group of clean-limbed young men, every one of whom was grimly intent on his graduation. Colonel Moore said:

" No one here questions your bravery, your willingness, your ability. That has never been the point at all. There is this, though: some of us who have faced this hard training are better fitted for other branches of the Forestry Service. The Department recognises that. ' Smoke jumpers' are beings apart; they must have a real love for the danger and the work. Others of you will be retained in the Service if you so desire. I want to make it clear that you who are not graduated in to-morrow's ceremonies are still in the Service—that is "—and he smiled—" unless you commit some misdemeanour in the meantime! "

They edged on their seats. He went on :

" We are graduating this batch ahead of time because you have been well trained and because you are urgently needed. You're to be assigned immediately. There are several fires in this area which call for immediate attention. Your work, if you are so assigned, will count as credits towards your graduation as full-fledged Rangers—or, if you prefer, 'smoke jumpers'—because Government regulations insist that active service take credit counts in place of academic service. We did the same thing during the recent War, at West Point. Now . . ."

The colonel's voice droned on ; important but not so important as what was to come.

" To those of you who are not qualified

as 'smoke jumpers' I want to bring a message. You are still in the Forestry Service of the United States Department of Agriculture and you have had long training at Government expense. To you, then, I say —there is work in the Service for all of you. Failure to make the grade as a 'smoke jumper' doesn't eliminate you from Forestry Service. When the lists are published I want you to give thought to the other activities you've been trained in and where you may serve. The big need right now is for men accomplished in reforestation and reseeding; cruising, marking timber; making range surveys and soil-erosion work—in nurseries and laboratories. There is a place for you all." Then he smiled. " But I still prefer a 'smoke jumper.' "

He stopped speaking and the meeting broke up. There was no more to be said. The lists were all out. The remainder was routine. Some time had to be expended for the purpose of completing the required number of hours in the course ; that was all. The rest, as Ladd Malcolm said, was "wrapped up and packaged."

" See you in a minute or two, Ladd," Rick said, and walked off, musing to himself. So it was about over. Now for the actual work! The work that he had lived for!

Malcolm had headed for the mess hall, where some of his fellows had gathered. Rick wanted a minute or two to think. He had halted when a voice spoke at his elbow.

" Dreaming, Rick? "

He turned swiftly. Molly. Molly Wayne. He had talked with her more than once ; in fact, wanted to say more than he had ever dared say. As niece of the Field Superintendent, Molly was an established personage hereabouts. She was more than that, though, to the cadets. She was an ideal.

Rick knew that she had specialised in social welfare and nursing. That she had wheedled their highest superiors, Colonels Wayne and Moore, the former her uncle, into finding a place for her here. He tried to keep the admiration out of his eyes when he returned casually—he hoped!——

"Yes, dreaming, Molly. Glad it's over and glad of the work ahead."

He felt her move closer to him, and her hand fell lightly on his wrist.

"You're cut out for it, Rick. I just stopped to say congratulations and wish you luck. I'm on duty—dispensary. So I'll say it—good luck, Rick Harding, smoke jumper!"

She moved swiftly away and shadows closed around her. He stood looking after her for a moment, his eyes taking on warmth, then he walked on, lost in his own thoughts.

CHAPTER THREE

RICK FINDS A MASCOT

THERE was another lecture that night. It was part of the course and no one especially wanted to attend it but it was obligatory. After changing, Rick surveyed the barracks where he had lived for so long.

He smiled, a warm little smile; he'd be leaving soon. Well, his training had brought something. It had brought knowledge of how to fight fire in the forest. It had given him a complete command of every agency known to science wherewith to combat the awful menace of fire.

Another speaker followed Colonel Moore, a retired officer in the Service who had seen distinguished duty in the recent war. He told them :

" One thing that has not been stressed enough, I think—especially in this north-west area where you are now stationed—is the all-out co-operation this service has with the men of the Canadian Government. We're right on the Border here. I wonder how many of you realise that this is the longest undefended borderline in the whole world? And aside from police, neither the Canadian nor the American Government has a fort or a soldier stationed here to defend the interior of the country against aggression. There is immigration, to be sure. Customs, naturally. But you'll never see an armed guard facing you when you cross the Line, never see a man with a club telling you to turn back. These two Governments have co-operated for many years, and in this service of ours they are working together hard. I bring this up merely to remind you, you graduates who are now entering the actual Service—if you need help, call on a Canadian servant ; if he needs your help, he'll know well enough he can call on you! "

Afterwards, " He's right, too," Malcolm said. " I wonder how many of us ever think of that—what he said. Probably the longest borderline anywhere in the world and all it means is that our two Governments work together."

They were walking towards the place known as the Coke Palace. It was a shabby but cool and friendly rendezvous for the cadets in their off-duty hours, a place where soft drinks could be had, sandwiches, hot dogs, and what went with them. Most of the cadets off duty—at least those having the wherewithal—dropped in nightly.

On the way Rick and Malcolm halted before the bulletin board. The board was plain under a low but clear light outside the headquarters office. It bore notices for the following day's work.

Most of the cadets had discarded jackets and were in soft shirts. Open collars were permitted in this season. A breath of air wafted the odour of soft drinks and mingled with the popcorn and frankfurter smell.

Rick stood with feet spread wide apart after he and Malcolm had elbowed their way in among the others, to read the orders ; he heard the varying comments from other cadets, and over it all came the sweet but tangy breath of the open. In the air was a hint of smoke. He saw his own name on a list and he saw Malcolm's too. He stared hard.

" They've got you and me and Brad Hovey in the same crew for to-morrow! "

Malcolm was exclaiming. "You say you were praying, Rick?"

Rick had seen, too. So, for part of a permanent crew, he was to be thrown in with his only enemy in the class! Brad Hovey.

"I love it!" he said dryly. "Come on!"

They made for the Coke Palace. Malcolm suddenly loosed an exclamation, and when Rick turned his companion was bent over a small tail-wiggling mongrel pup. The puppy must have had some schnauzer in him, because he was mostly grey and sported a very short tail and whitish-grey whiskers in a black face. He looked hungry. His tail was the most obvious thing about him.

"Looks like smoke!" Malcolm said. "Maybe he wants to join up—he's camouflaged for it all right! Come on . . ." Then he added, "Smoky!"

At the suddenly inspired name, the dog raised his head and uttered a sharp yap of pleasure.

"Smoky it is!" Rick agreed. "Let's feed him! I think he showed up to enlist! Maybe he'll bring us luck on the new job, too—I think we might need it. And he certainly doesn't seem to belong to anybody."

The pup didn't even have a collar. But for all that, he didn't look like a mongrel, not quite. That soft, yet wiry coat proclaimed his heredity somewhere. He cavorted, quite as if he belonged, into the Coke Palace, and his appearance was greeted with various comments from the cadets already installed in the booths or at the fountain.

The Coke Palace was smoky too. A babel of voices met the new arrivals, and it was hard to untangle the gist of the warring comments. Most of the cadets were speculating on where their orders would take them, on what the assignments on the board meant to them personally.

Rick was thinking: Hovey . . . Usually six or seven jumpers were assigned to each smoke-jumping plane, along with a crew chief or chief of operations. Rick had noticed that his boss on the crew was

Whelan, Duff Whelan, with whom he had served many times during training. Whelan had apparently been released from his duties as an instructor to regular duty, because of the emergency in the area.

Rick liked Whelan. Whelan was an old-timer, and had known Rick's father. He had been a Forestry Service Ranger for fifteen years before obtaining transfer to this present section. He was grizzled, hard, and tough. He had narrowed blue eyes and a snap-lock for a mouth. But he knew every part of his job. He must have been in his early forties, but he looked nearer thirty, a hard thirty and a grim one.

Behind the layers of smoke clouding the Coke palace, Rick's eyes found Hovey. Brad Hovey was in one of the booths farthest from the door, and three cadets were with him. Rick knew them all.

Smoky, newly christened, had decided he liked the place. A cadet reached out and treated him to half of a frankfurter on a roll. That vanished instantly. He had another bid, a piece of hamburger, from another cadet, while Rick and Malcolm were trying to find places not already filled by their fellow-cadets. That wasn't at all easy.

Finally Malcolm said, " You grab us a seat if you can locate one. Prowl. I'll dive in there and snatch us a couple of bottles. Yell when you see me comin', if you have any luck. Hey, Smoky, where——? "

He elbowed his way to the soft-drink bar. Rick surveyed the room. There was nothing unusual ; perhaps a little more hilarity to-night, on account of the release of orders and stations.

But the place was usually crowded at this hour.

Suddenly there penetrated a shrill " Yip! "

Rick turned. He did not know Smoky too well, but he knew dogs, and he knew that Smoky was the only dog in the place. He knew, too, that the tenor of that " Yip! " meant that Smoky was scared.

Something told him. He faced squarely

to where Brad Hovey was sitting. Hovey was laughing. The dog's head was imprisoned between his knees and a distance of two feet away from Smoky's head was the end of a hot-dog-on-roll that had been used for bait. Smoky yipped again.

Rick went striding through the layers of smoke, his eyes angry. He brought up in front of Hovey's booth conscious of the stares of the other jumpers fixed on him questioningly. The puppy wriggled free, pushing his paw against a sore nose.

Brad Hovey looked mockingly at Rick. Rick said, into the silence that his coming had caused :

" Lay off that pooch, Hovey! He may not have belonged to me yesterday but he did when I brought him in here. Get it? "

Hovey blinked and started to get up. His nearest companion put a hand on his arm, but he shook it off. He came erect and faced Rick Harding squarely.

" You talking to me, I reckon? "

" You can reckon or not! " Rick retorted.

" I was. I don't like to see dogs ill-treated."
He added, " Anybody's dogs! "

For an instant Hovey hesitated, as if he
meant to deny the inference. Then his eyes
clouded and he shook his head.

" I wasn't aiming to ill-treat the dog,
yours or anybody else's." he said. " Just
having a little fun. But if you're trying to
make a big point of it, let's say I was.
What next? "

The dog had scampered off, and Rick
could hear Ladd Malcolm scolding him,
somewhere behind him. No one was paying
much attention except those at the table.
But they were, plenty! A row in the cadets
corps was frowned on by the authorities.
These men had to work too closely together,
had to depend on one another too completely, for personal enmities to be allowed.

" That's all," Rick said. " Just that. Happens I like dogs—and it happens," he added
pointedly, " I don't like some people. Do
I get the idea across? "

Hovey sneered. " Sure do! And it goes

double! If that's all you've got to say, what's holding you here? "

Rick hesitated. He had seen Hovey's fists doubling up and now he realised that his own were clenched too. He could feel his shoulder muscles tightening.

A new voice cut in. Rick half-turned and Duff Whelan pushed in, hard and bulky. Whelan's eyes were frosty but knowing, when he said, " No trouble—not among my crew, I hope! " His voice was silky but none would have dared deny its import.

One of the men in the booth cleared his throat and said, " No, no trouble, Chief. Just talking about a—a dog." Then, with a relieved laugh, " Harding came over here to see a man about a dog! He's just going."

Whelan looked sharply at him and then at Rick ; under the look, Rick frowned and bent down to pick up the venturesome puppy, again at his heels. He stowed Smoky under his arm and moved to where Ladd Malcolm was elbowing his way through the press, his hands occupied with bottles of pop and food.

Malcolm waved towards a free table. Rick was glad enough to sink into a chair and become lost in the crowd.

Malcolm eyed him. "You and Hovey again?" he questioned, passing a cold bottle.

Rick nodded, still grim. "Yes. And we're on the same crew too." He shook his head. "Maybe he wasn't too wrong; maybe I was. Maybe he does like dogs. Well "—he reached down and pulled Smoky's ear—" we've got quite a stretch of time to find out in. How much do I owe you, Ladd?"

CHAPTER FOUR

GRADUATION

ASSIGNMENTS for crews were officially completed the following day. The ceremonies of graduation were unimportant and soon over, that night. After them, Rick found himself alone at the edge of the landing field, the barracks and official buildings behind him, staring into the night.

If only that thing out of his past had not been with him, he was thinking . . . This was the spot he had aimed at for years. The assignments were all made ; graduation was about over. He was set. But the past still haunted him.

How much did Brad Hovey know of it?

There was still that quiet and serene mood that fell over the field and campus with evening. Afar was the subdued roar of a motor. That seemed somehow part of it all. As much a part, now he had come to know the place and all it stood for, as the drooping elms and the quiet shaded streets of the town, the historic buildings each with its own tale, whispering of the past. Yes, his school days had been good. This place bred men, men to face danger and hardship. It bred friendship. It also could breed enmity, like Hovey's.

Rick breathed deeply. The air for the last

three days had held the taint of distant smoke. It smelled of balsam and pine too, since the wind had shifted. Pine and balsam, but the disturbing tread of smoke-poison was still in it.

He turned. This had been graduation night, he told himself again. They had been stamped as fully trained "smoke jumpers"; authority had stamped them. The rest was routine. Even to the speeches. Graduation over, the cadets were cadets on probation no longer.

To-morrow was to come a last day of "holdover training," designed to patch up any ragged spots the cadets might have missed—that, and to make sure they were letter-perfect in their jobs.

Rick sniffed the smoke and grinned to himself. He had read of scarred old battle steeds, who smelled powder smoke from afar and became restive. It was like that with him.

He remembered the significant words of the school's chief, at the end of the ritual:

" As I informed you, you are being graduated early because there is actual and immediate need for your services. It is not an unusual custom in Government institutions. I promise you, though, my friends—you'll be in action sooner than any of you have been expecting. Be ready for it. And good luck! "

So Rick was ready for the last day when it came. He wanted badly to make a jump that was not simply practice—over a real fire danger. Such a fire as must be burning somewhere close by. The radio was still relaying reports of it. There had been a stream of official-looking visitors too, lately, solemn and intent men.

" They're shooting us right into it," Ladd Malcolm said when he came up with Whelan, his eyes gleaming.

But Whelan said, " Don't forget it's not a game, Ladd. From here on out, it's for keeps! "

Rick thought of all this, surveying the parachute tower from the ground. He found it hard to keep his mind on these final items of training. He heard Whelan reading out the assignments for the final routines.

" . . . And Cadet Harding! Cadet Harding will make his jump, full equipment. He will then proceed to demonstrate operations and to simulate direction of operations in a danger area." Whelan paused to explain to the listening crews. " You will be given marks on your execution of this final phase. The marks will not affect your graduation, only your record."

Rick climbed the tall tower. It was a regulation lookout tower built by the school for just this purpose. Whelan, the school officials grouped near by and behind him, was directing :

" Wind as it is : north-west, close to ground. Fire as designated. Cadet Harding to leap, engage and operate. He will find acting 'volunteer' crews waiting. He will take charge and direct them in combating fire. Ready! "

Cadet Harding was ready. Ready? He'd been waiting for this moment for two years!

He climbed the endless steps to the platform atop the observation tower, his equipment tight against his back. On top, on the wide platform, sat three judges, field glasses in their hands, papers and pencils between their knees.

The top offered a view of the countryside almost as good as from a plane. Off there somewhere, past the grey mist that was part forest-fire smoke, lay Pinnacle, Rick's home town. That was where old Piney Lane held out, and his friend Jude Lincoln, the sheriff. In a day or two . . .

Rick found himself at the edge of the platform and reaching for the rip cord of his 'chute. The ring was in his fingers and he heard the word—" Take off! " as from a distance.

A moment later he was moving his feet against nothing but air and feeling the tightening of the harness on his back as he went swaying downward.

He could see a sea of upturned faces. He reached up, found the guide rope, and began to steer his great white cloud in the direction that had been indicated.

Only a small figure against the sky, the billowing of the great 'chute dwarfing him. The wind carried him across the tops of trees, past the second clearing, into the valley sloping towards the river beyond.

He began to come down faster, all the while manipulating the guy ropes so that he would be borne to a position fairly close to his destination. Already, he could make out a scramble of toy figures moving to come up with him, the splashes of crimson on tree trunks meant to indicate flames.

Then he was nearing the ground. He came swaying into the lower branches of a tall pine, heard something rip, caught sight of the running figures moving towards him.

A few yards from the ground he did a quick jerk, freed himself of his harness, caught hold of a tough branch to break his fall, and—goggles shielding his eyes and face

—plummetted to earth on both feet, only staggering a little from the speed of his last few yards of descent.

Instantly he was in operation. The "volunteer" fighters were nearing him. Rick found his heavy gloves, twisted to free the tank of flame-extinguisher on his back, pushed into the area of what was supposed to be flame.

It was simple enough. He had rehearsed it often. When the "volunteers" arrived he could hear his own voice commanding a backfire and then directing it.

He drew the asbestos suit closer about him and forced a way into the flame area.

Then he went to work. It was almost real, at that. His own voice grew hoarse but he could see, past the film on his protective goggles, the "volunteers" taking his orders and working smoothly at the area. The stream of extinguisher fluid came jetting forth and played over the edge of the fire spread.

Real smoke came drifting across the

scene, from a smudge under careful control. Rick waded into it until he stood in the heart of the fire area.

All this time his voice was carrying over his shoulder, directing operations for the men who were supposed to be local volunteers, behind him.

He could see only directly ahead of him. His head had been totally covered by the regular helmet that was like a football helmet and baseball mask combined into one. The helmet offset chances of injury as well as fire hazard.

Smoke wavered in front of him from the boiling smudge pots, blotting out the scene in spots. He forced himself deeper into the heart of it and his hose extinguisher played on. Behind him, he could hear the voices of his helpers and knew he had won to the core of the supposed fire.

Under his direction, the workers were using shovels and also forming a line of bucket-passers, drawing water from a shallow stream nearby. The entire scene was alive with action, yet it was all controlled and smooth.

At last, a whistle pierced shrilly and some- one shouted, " It's all over—recall! " And Rick knew he had completed his last test.

He threw off his helmet and felt the cool breeze on his flushed cheeks. The others were moving up, talking and laughing.

" So that's what you guys have to learn to do! " one of the local volunteers observed to Rick when they were plodding back. The volunteers had been made up mostly from men in the region, but a few of the younger cadets and trainees had been dispatched to furnish " backbone." Now everyone was talking at once.

Rick laughed. " That's one of the things! A real blaze and it'd be something else again! "

" You done all right! " someone said.

One of the men laughed. " It was close enough to it, anyway, for this pigeon! That equipment you got to carry——"

" It's heavy and it's hot, of course," Rick

said. " But mostly it's asbestos. Fire'd be a lot hotter! "

When he at last got back to the pickup truck two more men were readying to hop off the central tower. Rick went at once to divest himself of his paraphernalia. Then to the shower.

That night the bulletin board posted the names : Rick had passed among the top jumpers. Most of the others had done well, too. Only one cadet had failed in a good score and he was being passed on probation.

This was a fine feeling. Rick Harding was a full-fledged "smoke jumper" at last. Now for the rest . . .

CHAPTER FIVE

THE OLD STOREHOUSE

THE small town of Pinnacle, where Rick had spent his boyhood, lay below the spreading wings of the ship that was carrying him the following day. From the air it wasn't much. None of the others in the plane could feel the emotion that came over Rick Harding as he stood gazing down out of the bay at the spreading panorama unfolding below.

He was on patrol.

They had not taken long with assignments. The need for Forestry Patrol men was too real.

No diplomas had been handed out as yet. The class was still technically "in training." But it had been drafted for actual work. These smoke jumpers were actually on the Government payroll even if they hadn't been officially assigned. Usually there was an interim period between graduation and assignment, but this was an emergency. And no one objected.

Over his shoulder Rick could see Hovey. Brad Hovey was bending over a buckle in his parachute harness at the moment, but he had turned just in time. Only a moment before he had been staring at Rick. The pup—Smoky—was having fun rolling with the motion of the plane every time it hit a wind variation. Smoky had been officially adopted by this crew.

And Smoky liked it. He might not have been sure of what it was all about but he liked it. He was with friends and knew it.

Even so, he had a habit of edging around when Brad Hovey was near. Hovey had watched Smoky's arrival with eyes that brooded, but he said nothing. The other smoke jumpers had all welcomed the dog in a big way and that had silenced Hovey. For that matter Rick had noticed, with something of puzzlement, that Hovey's glances at the dog were not the glances of a man who hated animals. Hovey had seemed a little worried, as if trying to find an answer to something. But he had kept to himself.

The plane banked again, then zoomed, until the tops of the trees of the Preserve made a green velvet sea far, far below. At a word from a Ranger at the intercom, which directed movements of the ship from the pilot's cabin, the plane flattened out, made a wide bank, came in evenly and smoothly over the town of Pinnacle, to head for the great forest acreage just beyond.

" Once," Rick told Ladd Malcolm, " this was all private land—lumbering outfits. The Government still leases it out in big hunks to private operators. My father's friend— and mine—Piney Lane, is a sort of caretaker down there. Employed by a private holding company. Piney was a good lumberman once, I'm told. But he tackled one big tree once too often. Sure, he levelled the tree but he got himself caught in its fall and he's a bit crippled now. Still, nothing worries him! "

The grey eyes staring down were anxious. Wisps of white cloud strata whipped past the plane's nose, caressing its sleek sides. At moments the ground below was blotted out as they slipped into a cloudbank, to emerge instants later into sunshine.

Whelan turned up the intercom so that his voice could be heard through the length of the ship :

" We're cruising over a small blaze below. Not our assignment, but we're checking it. It's under control, I think—*they* think! We're using it as a practice field for a regulation jump. Crews will take off on the word, investigate, check damage and danger, then report to town of Pinnacle where truck will appear at five o'clock : dot. Understood? "

" Roger," came back the response from a dozen throats.

They moved in. The plane banked once more, then, at a word from Whelan, its nose pushed upwards and it soared until they were well over fifteen hundred feet. From that altitude the wisps of smoke from fires under control were no more than pale greyish splotches amid the great expanse of verdure.

The little town of Pinnacle slipped away.

The ship nosed down, eased, seemed to slow up in the air. Whelan's voice came again over the intercom :

" Crew! Number One Crew—bail out! "

They needed no further orders. Rick was

on the first crew. So were Ladd Malcolm and Brad Hovey. They stepped to the bay, adjusted goggles and 'chute harness, turned for a last look.

Rick saw Malcolm tumble overside. He followed the downward plunge for a moment, fascinated. Then Hovey was stepping off, without a backward look. Smoky came crawling up. Rick pushed him back. Whelan grinned at him as he caught the dog and pushed him out of the way. Rick stepped to the port opening, took a long look below, nodded, and stepped into space.

As always, it seemed a long time before the 'chute took over. He could almost tell when the small handkerchief on top of it— the flap that first caught the wind's updraft to tear loose the packaging of the parachute proper—took hold.

Then . . . that swift jerk and the tug, the slowing up of that mad downward rush, the easing of that empty feeling in the pit of the stomach—the 'chute opened.

Rick hung swaying there, playing with

Rick hung swaying there, working on the guide ropes.

the cords guiding him, trying to catch what wind there was to lift and draw him into the area to which he had been assigned. Below he could see boiling clouds of smoke.

Hovey must have already landed; he couldn't see him. But from the air he could see the town of his boyhood, lying there quiet amid its forested cradle of green hills. Only a mile more or less from the smoke-smudge.

Below now was the wide expanse of land that had once been patrolled by Piney Lane. Rick wondered if he'd find his father's friend down there somewhere. Piney kept his own cabin at the edge of the land he had worked over as caretaker for so many years.

The trees were suddenly rushing towards him, their tops waving at him as he swayed above them. The air still rushed past his face but not so rapidly; there was only breeze now.

Rick's feet brushed a treetop. He looked for his companions, but could see no one within his range of vision. Then he was plummetting down between the trees and working at the release of his 'chute.

He felt the silk above him catch a branch midway up a tall pine, felt the abrupt jerk. The ground below was carpeted with a layer of ancient leaves and pine needles.

Releasing himself from the 'chute, he dropped directly into a bed of fern, then quickly slipped free of his harness.

He stood there for a moment, listening. The woods held a deep and solemn hush. Overhead the mighty forest monarchs met with their heads somewhere between him and the sky, tall and strong and proud. The light below here was dimmer too. There was no sound at all.

But he had already marked the spot where a fire had been reported, and he trudged towards it.

His plodding footsteps made no sound on the thick carpet of old leaves and growth.

He came upon the fire—a small burn, a "smudge." He took mental notes of it for his report, decided it was a case of spontaneous combustion, then proceeded to work on it.

This was simple. His liquid thrower did most of the work. He had the satisfaction, after less than half an hour, of being able to walk straight across the blackened area in his fireproof boots. He then proceeded to examine the leaves of the trees nearest, the lower branches. Some of them had been singed but they were in no danger.

He stared upward, trying to see sky through the tall forest in which he stood. Only patches of it were visible.

The silence lay all about him, almost a sound in itself.

Rick tightened up his harness, and turned to make his way towards Pinnacle. He jerked the compass from his overalls. If other jumpers had landed nearby, he had not glimpsed them.

Along the way to Pinnacle every land-mark—even some of the old trees—re-minded him of his boyhood. He veered a little from his direct path and presently came

Hovey was sitting across from him in the swaying truck, and his eyes, fixed mostly ahead as he sat bracing himself to its pitching, came back to the pup now settled between Rick's feet.

The big motor burned up the shaky roads to the Base. Night had come completely and on every side there was a wall of darkness through which they were moving. No one talked much.

At last the low building surrounding the conical tower showed through the darkness. Then the truck was tearing in towards the headquarters building, its white headlights splaying over the field as it made the turn. It drew up and its occupants piled out. Already lights had come on all around them, and the field itself was bright.

Whelan took it in a single leap from his perch and went charging into the office. There was plenty of light there. The others leaped off the truck and scrambled for quarters, and new supplies. Rick headed for the quartermaster's with some others, to ask for and receive a brand-new parachute.

He slung it over his shoulder and then, as he walked, started to buckle on the harness. Malcolm was chattering.

"Must be a new area. Certainly not where we were to-day."

Rick agreed. "There've always been fires through here," he said. Then, "I can recall many of them. A small blaze is taken as run of the mill; mostly the local folks can take care of it. But there've been so many blazes started in these parts lately that I suppose Headquarters suspects anything at all. My guess is—incendiarism."

"You mean—folks deliberately starting fires?"

"Something like that. Only why—unless a guy's gone nuts? Or," he continued thoughtfully, brooding over it, "he might have a reason at that. He might just possibly be wanting to distract attention—the Department's attention—from what he was actually doing somewhere else!"

The crew piled out to the airstrip, where

a big plane was revving its motors, the roar of them drowning out all other sound. The crew streamed towards it.

Rick noticed that there was something other than amateurishness about the men he was with now. They did less talking, for one thing. They had had a taste of smoke and they were getting to know their jobs.

Then they were airborne, zooming out over the collection of buildings forming the Base, watching them dwindle into blackness almost in seconds. The plane's headlights cut through the dark as she took altitude, banking north and westward.

On the horizon there appeared a dull glow.

With the converted " Skymaster's " speed of almost two hundred and fifty miles an hour, its 1350 h.p. Pratt & Whitney engines drove hard through the blue night, and the miles below reeled away. The blaze was soon visible from the port, where the crew had grouped.

Against the night's velvet it looked like

a large blaze. It was northward of Pinnacle, but not so distant, Rick realised, as miles were reckoned on this frontier.

Malcolm started to say something. Rick looked down, grinned. Somehow Smoky had managed to get with them again. But Malcolm's words were drowned out in the roar of the motors and the rasp of Bard Hovey's harsh voice just behind them.

"Won't be any trouble now," Hovey was saying. "The heroes are here—and the pooch!"

Rick swung. But Whelan was close, staring out of the port on his own account. For an instant Rick and Hovey stared into each other's eyes, then Rick turned away.

"We'll get to settling things one of these days, Hovey," he said, and presented his shoulder.

There was little time for more. The mighty Pratt & Whitney's had been eating up the night sky in huge chunks. They all tensed as they felt the big ship tilt forward in a banking turn and circle over the fire area.

By now the fire was visible all right!

It made a circle like a crimson wedding ring cut out of the night's velvet black. An almost perfect circle. The core of the ring was an angry red and it was circled by ruby flame. The core looked as though it might be dampened, from the way the smudge showed—maybe a lake. There were hundreds of small lakes in this area.

The northern tip of the circle was burning furiously. Even from this height, men could be seen crawling about down below, amateurs at work trying to halt devastation.

Whelan picked up the intercom, held it close to his mouth. His eyes were intent. Then he dropped the instrument, letting it dangle, and turned to bark out:

"Ready to jump!" An instant. "Stations!" Then he added, as they scrambled, "Two at a time, work in pairs. You know

what to do when you get down there. Okay
—let's go! "

Two men bailed out immediately as the
plane circled, waiting until decently below
to jerk the rip cords of their 'chutes. Then
two more. When Rick stepped to the bay
he found that he and Brad Hovey were coming up together.

For an instant they glared at each other,
then Rick turned away and stepped off into
space. Hovey was behind.

The night beneath was ebony-black and
the crimson ring of flame only made it the
blacker. The plane was banking again,
winging over for a second drop.

Rick fell fast. He counted, finding it hard
to count, then jerked his 'chute release. By
that time he was heading for the earth
head-first.

Slowly his body straightened out as the
rushing downward plunge increased. Trees
and smoke and red gleam of fire all came
mounting towards him at once. He clutched
the rip cord.

He had lost track of Hovey, but overhead he could hear the plane banking for a new drop.

He felt the brush of taller trees against his face, let himself go. The parachute clung to some outstretched hostile branches, dragged a minute, snapped, and then came free. Rick slashed at his harness, slipped loose, dropped about ten feet to a carpet of fern and moss, and plunged instantly towards the crimson glow ahead.

It became more marked as he approached. Coming up, he was able to see that it had begun in a low, isolated hut standing at the edge of what was, on closer approach, not lake but a large pond. It was like a care-taker's hut—and by this time it was almost consumed by flame.

Rick went to work. To avoid spreading, he started a small backfire, nursing behind it to keep it moving in the wind, which was —luckily—behind him.

He stepped past the backfire and towards the core of the flame. A shrill *Yip!* came at his heels. He turned, lifting the protective mask and visor, to shout :

" Smoky! How in blazes did *you* get here? "

He had an answer oddly enough. A voice from the dark behind him jeered, " Thought you couldn't be separated from him, Harding! I brought him down, under my pack! "

It was Hovey. Hovey standing with feet braced apart and his features twisted by the reflected glow from the fire.

Rick began to speak, then stopped ; he wanted to say a lot, but all he said was, " If it's your idea of fun, let's have it. Right now we've got something to do. Let's get at it! "

" You're not giving orders here! " Hovey snapped.

Rick looked at him, turning half-way from the spot he had selected to go to work on first. He said evenly, surprised at his own curbed temper, " That's right, Hovey, I'm not. I'm only doing my job. How's about you taking care of yours? "

He plunged on. The backfire he had begun was already taking hold, and he had the wind in his favour. It was not much of a wind but such as it was, it helped ; it fed the backfire towards the bigger blaze beyond.

For a long time the fight was hot. Rick was able to glimpse Hovey at intervals, past his clouded mask and the swirl of damp smoke that was coming up, it seemed, even from the ground itself. Rick was thinking. Once he could hear Smoky's *Yip!* Then he was back at his task. The stream of liquid from his tank of fluid went streaking into the bush. He could see that the backfire had narrowed the ring of flame on the north side of the blaze, so that he and Hovey had only the central area to contend with.

The scorch of the blaze penetrated through the heavy garments he wore ; it went past the asbestos gloves and the insulated shoulders of his suit. He moved like a man from Mars, in some strange motion picture, a weird, ungainly, lopsided figure amid clouds of white and black smoke splotched with crimson.

The flames slowly became subdued. Out past the smoke Hovey was working too; Rick could see the stream of his extinguisher hose playing on the fire near to where the small cabin stood.

He worked his way towards the cabin—and his suspicions came to a head. The fire had begun right here!

Incendiary, perhaps. Carelessness, at the very least. But that was not all—what were trespassers doing in this remote area? It was logging stand, timber growth entirely. Except for the small hut already ruined past help, it had nothing to do with the affairs of men.

The dog yipped at Rick's heels once again, the sound cutting into his thoughts. By now the ring of fire was narrowing down considerably. Then he and Hovey were face to face—their eyes gleaming at each other through the smoke.

" You'll play your little games once too

jump down and fight fires, maybe," Whelan said one night, three days after the last night alarm. " But I can make guesses, along with everybody else. Fires are still breaking out, and they're not explained. The patrol north of here has been alerted and that's why we've had a day or two of rest. But it's taken for granted, now, that there's incendiarism behind all this rash of blaze. Maybe not every blaze, no, but more of them than usual. The thing is . . ." He broke off, glanced at Rick and frowned.

" I know what's on your mind, Chief," Rick said, nodding. " I think I mentioned it to you before. What's behind all the freak blazes we're getting in this area? They can't all be carelessness, or even spontaneous combustion. Law of averages says no. And all these folks coming and going around here with buttoned-up mouths, they're busy wondering too. That what you're thinking? "

Whelan nodded. " I'm not paid to think, but—yes. And you did bring it up before, didn't you, Rick? Me, I like my job and I like to keep busy, but it sure looks like somebody in this area is making plumb sure I can't complain about idleness! Why? "

That was it. The others spoke of it too. The following days were anything but idle!

Continuous patrols. Then the patrols were nothing but curtain-raisers to the first big night alarm.

Molly met Rick outside the Coke Palace early one night. As always, she was trim and wistfully, darkly beautiful—to him anyway. He offered her a Coke, but she was on her way to her duties and refused.

" Not to-night, Rick," she said. " I'm busy till midnight, I guess." Then, " There's something stirring under the surface around here. Have you felt it? "

He frowned. " I've had the idea for a long time but I've had nobody to talk to about it. It all comes down, I guess, to the way everybody shuts up like clams any time mention is made of a possible purpose back of all these fire breaks."

She nodded. " Yes. It's that—and more too." In her position, Molly was likely to hear a lot of things, Rick knew. She wouldn't have had to try very hard either. Her dark eyes clouded now.

" You spoke up once, Rick," she said thoughtfully. " You asked them all what could lie behind the outbreaks. You never did get an answer, did you? But you've noticed the official-looking visitors we've been having lately? The District Super-intendency is investigating. They know that, even allowing for accidents, this area is facing something peculiar, something no one can put a finger on."

" Have *you* any ideas? "

" No." He thought how pretty she was when she frowned that way. " No," she repeated. Then quickly, " You have, though! Haven't you? "

" I've tried to offer my ideas. And Piney Lane has a few too. What it comes down to is we're asking if the strangers in these parts can be looking for something. And doing damage while they look. But looking for what? "

She didn't answer that. Molly had heard too. And she knew they were both thinking of the same thing, only neither of them would put it into words.

The vanished Fund. The mystery that had survived for so many years. He mentioned Piney Lane again and the two strangers he had seen in Pinnacle, Bull Ventner and the sullen Jeff Cadre.

Molly seemed to want to say more but she bit it back as if she had thought better of it. They didn't know each other too well, Rick was thinking. She probably knew Brad Hovey as well as she knew him. Molly bent over to fondle Smoky's ears when the dog suddenly appeared at Rick's heels.

" I must go now," she said. " I think we'll find the answers somewhere, Rick." And flashing Rick a warm smile, she turned away from Smoky. " Sorry I can't join you. Be careful at the Palace. Good night Rick."

He stood watching her as she walked

towards the emergency dispensary attached
to the hospital in the rear of the Administra-
tion Building. Above her reared the tall
tower, the beacons. Past all that lay darkness. Smoky gave a little whine, then decided he'd stay where he was, after all,
though he had a fondness for Molly. Rick
grinned down at him and Smoky was at
his heels as he pushed his way into the
Palace.

Inside, the usual crowd had thinned out a
little. Someone offered the information that
a " rec " patrol had taken off about twenty
minutes before, adding, " More rumours.
Folks in this area are gettin' just plain
jittery."

Rick lost Smoky for a minute. He went
to the bar to pick up a bottle of pop,
frowned over the appetising-looking frank-
furters between their mustarded rolls, decided he wouldn't let himself be tempted,
then looked around for the dog.

The puppy was having a wonderful time.
Across the room he sat facing Brad Hovey,

a big hamburger sandwich half in and half out of his mouth.

Just then Ladd Malcolm came up, to range alongside Rick, and he saw too. Hovey had been bending over the dog. The next instant his head lifted and he was staring across at Rick.

Rick saw the challenge in the look, but he turned away. It was Malcolm who called, " Thought you didn't like dogs, Hovey. Those sandwiches cost money! "

Hovey sat back. " It's not dogs I dislike," he said. " Dogs are what their masters make 'em. Smoky and I got off to a bad start. We're friends now."

In a way it was an apology, but it had something of a smirk in it too. Malcolm said nothing. Not about that. What he did venture was plain business.

" I dropped into the ' Rec ' Hall for a minute and stayed to listen," he said. " Colonel Moore was there, talking about a new method we're picking up. It's called ' prescribed burning.' You have to work

with the fire towers, then work to the lee
side of your danger section and burn slowly
to meet the blaze. Sounds like a new name
for backfiring. But the colonel said they're
having a lot of success with it in New
Jersey, Mount Misery range. And they've
worked it successfully in Lebanon State
Forest Preserve too."

" I studied a pamphlet on it," Rick said.
" They've named it the RX : B System. A
couple of men walk along the edge of a
section dragging gasoline fire torches behind
them. They leave spots burning as they
pass. Then, when the section is surrounded
by what they call ' controlled flame' they
quarter that with a new set of torches and
burnings. And they keep on dividing it
into smaller sections, attacking each one
separately. I doubt if we could use it, but
it's something to know. We're emergency
boys. That's a great development, but it
comes either after or before we've done our
job."

" Some of the newer lads are transferring

to that work," Malcolm said. "Me, I like what we do best."

Rick agreed. "The other's important but not as exciting. Here's a Coke. Sandwich?"

"Not now." Ladd gurgled thirstily. "Funny around here when there's no excitement. Saw you and Molly talking. She's a swell gal."

Rick nodded. He didn't want to talk about Molly. It was disturbing, the feeling he had about her. She was a favourite with all the crew but towards him there was a certain shyness he wondered at. And he wondered at his own feelings too.

He was still pondering it, talking back at the more talkative Ladd Malcolm in monosyllables, when the alarm hit them. Odd, he told himself when the big siren screeched out, he'd been expecting it right along. Somehow he had known there would be work for them all to-night. Somehow he'd known the day's work hadn't ended.

The sound came screeching across the open, a banshee wail, rising and ebbing to rise again. Lights flashed on all over; the big tarmac became a blinding apron of white.

Rick turned to look for Smoky. But the dog had scuttled out as quickly and eagerly as one of those Dalmatians he had read about in the days of horse-drawn fire engines.

Smoky didn't know much about it, but he knew that, if he could help it, he wasn't going to be left behind.

Brad Hovey went pelting through the door. Ladd Malcolm gulped the remains out of his Coke bottle and set it down on the bar. Rick followed suit.

They were all shoving through the door then, the door jammed with talking, speculating smoke jumpers on the qui vive.

Rick found himself in the dark, a darkness whitened by the field lights, which were throwing great beams of refracted radiance into the heavens. The bull-throated roar of motors came. Men ran crazily here and there. Rick lost Malcolm and headed for the barracks and his equipment.

He almost collided with Molly, emerging from the dispensary. She had to steady herself by his arm for a moment.

"No rest for the smoke jumpers tonight!" she said. "I'm just as glad I didn't come with you for your drink of pop. I'd have had to finish alone, wouldn't I?"

"Must be a bad alarm, and plenty sudden." Rick frowned. "Listen to that siren!"

She stood holding on to his arm and it was only then that he looked down and noticed that. In the glow from the field, she was a small, gallant figure, her dark hair tumbling over the cape she had slung over her shoulders. Rick could feel his pulses stirring.

She turned quickly to him then, a little breathless. "It's almost back where you were last time, Rick," she told him. "Some-

where around Pinnacle. Maybe—maybe
your ideas——"

"Maybe they're not so crazy, after all!"
he finished for her. "Somebody's nosing
around there, looking for something. We
had that whole area quiet when we left, I'll
swear to that!"

"It was Piney Lane who called in the
alarm," Molly said. "I was there, and I
remembered your speaking of him. He's
not an excitable man, is he?"

"He's anything but!" Rick said. "I'll
be off, Molly. You see my pooch?."

She drew back. "Scuttling at Brad
Hovey's heels!" She laughed. "Maybe
hoping to find you that way. Good luck,
Rick!"

When she moved off, she stood for a
moment looking after her. Seeing the trim
lines of her graceful young figure, the way
her cape came floating back gaily, the way
her lithe, springing steps carried her.
What had she told him? Yes—Piney Lane
had called in the alarm. Strange things

were happening in this district these days !

The Service plane loomed up big and mountainous across the field. Men were hurrying towards it from all directions.

Rick tumbled inside the barracks and found his extra equipment in a hurry. He whirled and went pelting out with it, struggling into parts of it as he ran. He jerked the extinguisher over his back and fumbled with his harness, stumbling towards the plane.

He collided with two other smoke jumpers as he reached the side of the plane. They were laughing, talking fast, alert if ever a crew had been alert. Whelan was barking commands, checking his crew as the individuals came up. Rick found the ladder that had been dropped down.

Whelan was sweating. He bent over, eyes scanning the equipment Rick carried, checking it.

Rick said, " It's all here Chief, even if I did dig in a hurry. Pinnacle again, eh? "

"Around there," Whelan replied. "Maybe we should change our base to right inside that town of yours. We're gettin' to know it's on the map anyhow. Get along!"

CHAPTER NINE

RICK TAKES COMMAND

RICK stepped into the belly of the ship. Most of them were ahead of him. Malcolm said, " Come to think of it, this ought to be our first actual night alarm.

Not practice, I mean. Ought to be real hot stuff."

"Fires usually are," someone said, with a laugh.

The motors revved louder. It was necessary to cup a hand to the ear of the next man and shout in order to make yourself heard.

But the inside of the great carrier was orderly. These men had been trained for this. Extra 'chutes hung from racks, extra asbestos suits, all aligned. Racks held extra extinguisher tanks too. The seats ranged along both sides of the big ship, and above them the rounded ceiling curved over to form shadows.

Outside, voices sounded, then were lost in the roar of the engine. The great propellers split apart the night in their fierce rage. The white lights cut through the dark and reached for the farthest hills. The ground crew was turning the wings to meet the head-on wind for the take-off.

They could hear the last great roar as the engines churned, then the blocks were released. They started moving, gathered speed. The plane wobbled a little as it taxied down the long runway. They all knew when its wheels left the tarmac and the sensation of being in the air came. One or two of the men moved to the bays. The rest tried to yell at each other.

It was only as they levelled out that Rick caught sight of Smoky. Whelan had let out a roar almost competing with that of the motors, but it was too late. Hovey was standing there looking stubborn. Rick could see his lips moving towards whatever it was Whelan was saying. He could even hear Whelan's bellow:

" Dogs don't climb ladders! Not without help they don't, and somebody had to carry him up that ladder! Unless he's better than me—I had to climb the steps! "

But Whelan evidently decided to forget about it. There was nothing to be done anyway. The plane by this time was four or five thousand feet above the earth, hurtling through the blue-black night like some monster out of another age, its forward beams piercing the gloom for a long way ahead.

" Pinnacle! It's Pinnacle again! " came someone's shout as the plane tipped and the rush of wind permitted fragments of speech to be heard. Then another voice : " What's that town Pinnacle got that no other place has? "

Rick could hear that much, though he couldn't distinguish the voices. Even so, one or two of the jumpers must have sensed something, because they looked towards Rick and then away fast. Rick busied himself with testing his equipment.

Smoky was rolling with the plane's motion. He sighted Rick and came unsteadily towards him. He looked up at Rick and his dark eyes seemed to be begging forgiveness. Absently Rick pulled his ears.

The big carrier went roaring on through the night. A blaze was sighted northward of its destination and the plane veered in that direction but soon banked again to come in over the area surrounding the village of Pinnacle.

It wasn't long, not with the speed they were making, before the real blaze was in view. Whelan pushed to the bay and stared down, then reached behind him for his binoculars.

Over his shoulder, he roared, "Somebody's down there already. They've started cuttin' lanes. But it'll take more than that with the start it's got. This one, so help me, was started by hand. I'll take bets on that! It's too well planned and it's got too big a start."

Ladd Malcolm heard that and shouted at Rick. "This time we get a real work out!"

Rick nodded. "We'll make it." He added, "Nobody can tell me these aren't incendiaries. Maybe not all of them in this area but this one below anyway. Why, the towers, with the alidade reporting system, could have spotted this before night if there'd been any sign of it. It means that someone started it and made sure it got headway in a hurry."

" But why? " Malcolm looked puzzled.

" Maybe," Rick mused out loud, " to draw us off the real target. If we're busy here, we can't be patrolling somewhere else, can we ? And maybe seeing things we shouldn't."

Malcolm frowned. His puzzlement showed in his young open features. Then he laughed. " If that's it, all we've got to worry about is—where *don't* they want Government Rangers to be! Because we're ' Government,' no matter what else we are. And official too."

" I had that in mind," Rick said, and turned to play with Smoky, who had tired of it forward and was seeking his earlier loyalty, it seemed. Smoky looked as though he knew he had no business here.

But the dog wasn't to blame. Smoky loved this and he'd take any chance he had to get into it. Rick knew it. Rick also knew that Brad Hovey had worked it, mostly to irk him.

Ladd Malcolm braced himself as their carrier banked once more. They were circling now, circles that were narrowing more and more. Below them the fire devastation lay fully visible. Whelan went stumbling forward to the pilot's cabin.

" Brad Hovey's kind of sweet on Molly, I noticed. And Molly's been actin' real nice to you lately, Rick."

Rick felt himself flush. " Brad Hovey started this riding before we ever knew Molly. She wasn't based here when we came; she got her transfer later on. Anyway, it isn't Molly. Hovey doesn't need an excuse to play dirty ball."

" I can't think he feels he's playing dirty ball," Malcolm said. " It's just—well, call it pure cussedness. I don't think, even if I don't go for him in a big way, that Brad Hovey's bad inside."

Rick turned away. " If he is, it'll show

up on this job of ours. For my part, the jury's still out! "

That was it. With Rick, the " jury was still out." He didn't actively dislike Hovey and there was some question in his mind as to whether Hovey really disliked him as much as he appeared to. Molly Wayne was not the answer; at least, she wasn't all the answer. Her favours were pretty impartially given out. She was a friend, that was all. If she seemed to have a secret, unspoken sympathy for him, Rick Harding was certain it didn't show for anybody else to see. Molly was a favourite and they all liked her.

But Hovey was going out of his way to be unfriendly. There might not even be a plausible explanation ; maybe it was one of those cases of a natural enmity between men. It had happened before. Rick wasn't aware of any feeling of enmity, only of resentment, but Hovey might have other feelings. Or maybe Hovey wished he had seen Smoky first and adopted him. Maybe he was a real dog lover in spite of appearances, and was jealous of Rick on that score.

The plane circled again, nosed down, nosed up, then Whelan came slamming out of the forward compartment, to yell over the intercom, his voice carrying even above the roar of the big motors: " Okay—stations! Number One Crew, set—at bay! Number Two ready! Number Three stand by! "

Rick was on Crew Number Two. So were Hovey and Malcolm.

They readied. They aided one another in getting the extinguisher tanks strapped into place, tested each other's gear. Rick could see Smoky weaving now with the plane's more erratic motion, and he grinned. Smoky might be sorry for his disobedience before he was through. The scene below looked plenty warm.

Looking down, Rick called Malcolm's attention to a strip already burned out. A " burned area." . . . That meant the regular Forestry Patrol men had already marked the spot; that they had been here before and started counter-measures to check possibilities. From the clouds the place looked like a good home for " flash fires," another name for fires beginning by themselves due to spontaneous combustion.

Whelan's voice came again : " Number One Crew—bail out! "

Rick stood back, his eyes narrowed, watching the first batch crowd the bay, get themselves checked, and take off. When the ship made a lower circle they began to drop out. Whelan was watching too.

" Number Two Crew! "

Rick stepped into position. He was nearest the bay, anyway. And he didn't want to jump too close to Hovey. Malcolm was alongside him, his eyes glistening with eagerness.

Then it came : " Number Two Crew—bail out! "

Rick stepped off first, aware of Malcolm just at his elbow. Far below the red light of the fire was a blur. He dropped into a well of space, found himself twisting as he plunged, felt the sweat on his palms as he readied for the 'chute release. Then he saw he was almost over his objective and let go.

The 'chute seemed to be ages in catching. Rick closed his eyes and continued to plummet down head-first into darkness, darkness lighted only moments later as instinctively he jerked the release and felt the first wavering cessation in his speed earthward. An instant afterward the pilot handkerchief caught and the big folds of the umbrella over him began to blossom out.

He still sped earthward at a tremendous speed. The night air rushed past his face, laved the sweat on his body.

He opened his eyes more fully to see the fire ring below. At the same time the 'chute caught hold and his mad career downward lessened.

A second later he was floating, the 'chute billowing high and white against the blue night sky.

Under his feet, which were treading air, the scene commenced to take shape.

He worked the rope controls of his carrier, catching the wind drift in order to manœuvre for his landing spot . . .

Then he was able to make out the blaze. From the air he could see midget figures. One or two Rangers, but mostly volunteers from Pinnacle, he guessed. They had already made fire lanes.

Then he saw what was more important, something those on the ground could not hope to see, because they lacked the advantage of height. The fire extended over a large enough area to be termed a bad one, but actually it had centred in one spot, and the Rangers below weren't fighting that spot yet.

Rick knew that his brother smoke jumpers would see what he was seeing, that weak spot in the raging crimson demon below, and they would manœuvre to land somewhere near the core, just as he was doing at the moment, praying that the wind would aid him somewhat. But the wind seemed bent on carrying him away from his target. He worked harder on the guide ropes.

As he came lower, Rick felt himself being forced still farther away from his destination. He lunged at the ropes. Now he was able to make out the volunteers below him, ant-like figures against the crimson blaze.

The fire itself was a weird-looking spectacle by this time, made even stranger by the criss-cross of fire lanes that had been cut by patrolling Rangers; from the air they formed patterns like a game of hopscotch. There was no sign of his fellow-jumpers. But Rick put this down to that fact that, even slightly above him, a jumper would not be visible because of the wide expanse his 'chute made overhead.

Now he could make out the arena he was drifting into.

The fire fighters below were having all they could do to survive and try to check the roaring blaze. He could see the core of the fire clearly now, and the separate blazes seemed to be spreading out from it.

Rick's toes brushed a tall tree-top ; he felt it, even if he couldn't see it, because immediately below him the blackness was deep and there was slight chance of judging his exact distance from the ground.

He had to use his best judgment. The downward movement checked ; the 'chute caught, tugged, came free. The wind no longer had it in control.

Rick tightened his mask and goggles, wary of outflung branches. He felt the final jerk, another tearing rip, and let himself loose from the silk—keeping his toes pointed firmly downward to break the force of his fall.

He fell among a bunch of men all running in his direction. They stopped, regarding him as though he were an apparition.

There were five or six of them, all dirty and smoke-smeared. They wore nondescript clothing, burned here and there in patches. One of them was brushing at sparks on his checked shirt even as he sighted Rick.

Rick called out : " Forestry Patrol—from the Base! " He moved towards the men who were still standing staring at him. Then they began to understand and grins split apart the smoke-blackened faces.

" I take it you fellows are volunteers," Rick called. "My crowd is dropping in now . . . Supposing you take orders—just for the time being? I've had a chance "— gesturing towards the tangle of harness about his 'chute which was dangling from a tree limb—" to get a look at this from ' upstairs.' How about it? "

They were volunteers all right. One of them, seemingly the spokesman, said, "Glad you got here ; hope the rest of your crowd shows up. We heard you were on the way —Piney Lane phoned in for some help. And, boy, do we need it! "

" You ought to know me," Rick Harding said. He told them his name, watching their

varying reactions. " I was raised in Pinnacle.
Anyhow, let's get to work."

" Sure we know you, Harding," one of
the volunteers said. " I knew your paw.
What'll we do? "

Rick took over leadership then. These
men knew of him ; they must know of his
training too. That would give them con-
fidence. This was their own land too,
menacing the things they would always
fight to preserve. No matter what they
might think of that ancient story, they
could recognise that here was a man
trained to do the work they'd been trying
to do themselves. The rest didn't
matter.

Rick directed two of the men to locate
sand pits and find shovels to throw earth on
the blazes. Another he sent quartering for
water when the man said a stream was
" hard by."

Rick set them to making lanes in the fire
spread and attacking each patch thus segre-
gated separately, using extinguishers or

sand or just plain beating at it with dampened rags.

He himself stayed only long enough to direct operations. Then he pulled down his helmet, adjusted the goggles, and, loosing the extinguisher from his back, waded into the heart of the flames.

CHAPTER TEN

THE RESCUE

ALL about Rick the mighty forest had
taken on a new and dreadful look.
This menace that was eating at the great

135

arches of woodland was both man's enemy and nature's.

The fire might have been a " flash " to begin with, but it had had its origin in more than one spot. The crimson flames roared up in unexpected places, to eat at the vault of tall trees lifting overhead ; approaching a green bush and destroying it in one quick flash—a flame that struck suddenly and seemed to blow up with its own viciousness, like an explosion.

For a long moment Rick found himself standing still, marvelling. He had never imagined anything quite so weird as this. For seconds the clouds of smoke went billowing away from in front of his goggles and he had a view of the fire in front of him.

He stood staring down a wide avenue of tall trees, all alight in either their top or lower branches. The fire came rushing at them like a great red beast ; it stripped the dancing leaves in angry rushes of breath ; it scorched and seared the mighty trunks.

It was pitiful to see the forest monarchs

so utterly helpless in the face of its fury—the great boles confronting the sea of flame and then withering in seconds before its fiery breath. The leaves wiped out, with the branches, in a wave of flame that came and evaporated in the same instant, leaving only black destruction in its wake.

Yes, this was the enemy!

Rick could hear the voices of his crew behind him. He caught glimpses of some of his brother smoke jumpers as he went wading into the core of fire, his extinguisher working now, cutting at the fire with its own brand of savagery, facing its fury down with a fury of its own.

These patches must be isolated. Attacked one at a time. Rick forgot the heat and the danger, remembering only his own anger, an anger as real as the flames he was challenging.

But they were winning, he and his volunteer crew. And Rick had the satisfaction of knowing that he was being aided by his own fellows fighting the flame at other fronts near his own, checking and backfiring, as he was doing. If they had not been there, he would have had small chance. The jumpers had arrived in the nick of time, but even so they were having a tough job of it.

Somewhere off to the right and left, and probably even behind, they were at work, drawing part of the menace away from his front. Rick himself knew that he had located and attacked the core.

He knew something else too. He became more and more certain, as the fight wore on, that this especial fire was of man's making. He could tell it by the way the separate spots had been started all with some plan behind them. Some *human* enemy had teamed up with man's ancient enemy—fire.

He had penetrated far into the core by this time. Through his clouded goggles he could watch the extinguisher liquid working on the nearest, most vicious flames. It cut down flame like a cup of water on a burning matchstick, erasing it. Still, there were more patches. Rick, in the very centre of the core, was almost encircled by a ring of flame.

His goggles cleared and he made out another smoke jumper just ahead of him. He couldn't identify him, though. He could see the fluid from his extinguisher go jetting out at a great bushy clump, then die away.

Then the jumper turned, and Rick wanted to cry out. But he knew his mask would prevent sound carrying that far.

Just in the rear of the unknown smoke jumper a perfect circle of mingled alder clumps and pinon and juniper burst into flame without warning. The sudden "flash" picked up-wind, with the result that the jumper up in front was surrounded by fire.

Rick himself faced a new burst from directly behind him, and he had to whirl to battle it, relying on his tank of fluid, the flame-extinguisher that was his heavy cannon.

It was hot, desperate work for a long fifteen minutes. Step by step he moved forward, battling the menace threatening to create a new fire front. Then it was over.

Rick reeled away from the burned area he had forced under control, now crimson ash and charred timber. He wanted badly to take off his helmet, to gasp pure air, to gulp cool water.

He felt dizzied and weak. " I must have inhaled some carbon, after all," he told himself dully.

He propped himself against a large tree bole and allowed himself a moment of rest, gulping great lungfuls of air. It came to his throat strained, hot. His eyes misted. All around him the smoke swirled and eddied, still vengeful, still angry.

Then he felt something touch his right knee. He jerked quickly, his senses warning him of fire close by. But when he looked down it was not flame he saw—it was Smoky!

Something about Smoky warned him. There was no apology about the dog this time. Instead, he was trying to tell him something!

Rick bent down. He caught the dog's head between his hands and saw that Smoky had come in contact with fire. The wiry hair was singed in more than one place.

Smoky yipped pitifully. Then his strong teeth got a hold on Rick's pants and Rick came straight as the dog jerked insistently at his leg. His mind still dazed, he stared down questioningly.

Then suddenly he understood! Smoky was trying to urge him forward.

It was all there in the dog's movements, in the frenzied plea that amounted almost to words in the red-rimmed eyes.

Rick stiffened, found his hose, came erect. " Smoky! " he cried. Then, " Lead on, pup—to whatever it is! "

A few minutes later he found " it."

Smoky had understood his master's decision and had taken it for granted that Rick would come with him. He'd given a last triumphant *Yip* ! and darted off.

Weakened as he was, Rick was hard put to it to follow the bouncing form cavorting ahead of him so eagerly. Now he'd got his message across, Smoky was impatient.

Rick felt a little better for his rest. He swung his fluid tank around to where it would be instantly available, then plunged on at the dog's heels through the smoking, burning brush. Most of it in this section had been cleared, but a great patch of flame was roaring a little farther on.

Rick made for this, knowing it must be what the dog wanted him to do. It was. Instantly Smoky left off his urging and pranced ahead, turning from time to time to make sure he was being followed.

A moment later Rick forced himself through a thick cloud of black and white smoke that came from burned pine stands and young pine.

Brad Hovey was lying there, prostrate. In spite of helmet and uniform, Rick knew it must be Hovey. For one thing, Hovey had always affected an insignia of his own. Just above his belt line was a black swastika. He'd said it was an East Indian sign of good luck.

Well, he'd need luck now, Rick thought, ploughing in for the stretched-out figure.

There seemed to be little life in Brad Hovey. Rick knelt beside him. He saw the mask had slipped but that otherwise Hovey was equipped. His " thrower " lay a few feet away.

He was breathing with difficulty.

Rick noticed his hands—and understood. Hovey had been felled by a blow on the head—the giant branch broken off the blasted tree lay within two feet of him. It had brought Hovey down almost unconscious and then he had fought for air, in a dim, half-aware state, and had been trying to rip away his oxygen mask. He had succeeded enough so that the mask was half off and smoke had been seeping under it. Hovey was lying there breathing smoke, had been lying there for some minutes, helpless and unconscious.

Rick bent down and adjusted the mask. Then, while Smoky yipped his approval, he caught Hovey in a fireman's lift and threw the limp form over his shoulders. He was weak himself, but he knew he had to get the man out of this smoke-filled patch.

Blindly then, he followed Smoky. The dog was running on ahead—as if, Rick thought dully, he knows where he's heading!

Smoky did, apparently. For, weaving and staggering, Rick brought up a little later, knees touching the ground with the weight of the burden on his back, at the edge of a tiny stream that had become lost in the holocaust. He propped Hovey's body against a trunk and headed for the stream.

It might have been ages later, for he had lost count of time. The whole world had turned into a crimson inferno swirling with black smoke. He knew he had worked over

Hovey, though. And once he had stopped to lap at the water himself.

It was a nightmare. The water and the emergency flask every jumper carried worked together. At last he saw Hovey's eyes flutter open. They stared at him for a long moment with an unbroken disbelief in them—then Rick heard voices and felt himself getting giddy.

He grinned into Hovey's eyes—and abruptly toppled over.

The voices blended, fogged, took on bodies. Then he forgot them.

But he heard them again on awakening.

Whelan was there. And Piney Lane. There were others too, two of them men Rick remembered leading into the blaze at the beginning. He could hear Hovey's voice, then he slipped away into blankness again as he felt water at his lips, cold water . . .

Propped against a tree trunk waiting for transportation to come up, Rick saw, much later, that Hovey was lying near him. Hovey was staring about him in a puzzled way. There were a good many people about. Forest Rangers and men from town.

The remains of the flash fire seemed to have been subdued. There remained a small glow in the sky off to the north, but the smell of wood smoke had thinned into that faint odour of fire defeated : it hung over the little glade in which he and Hovey were lying.

Rick raised his eyes. All the many shapes seemed parts of the nightmare through which he had been walking. One big shape separated itself from the rest and then Piney was bending down over him. Rick put a hand to his forehead. Piney squatted in that familiar way he had, favouring his bad leg.

"I don't remember much," Rick told him. "But I'm glad a lot of people got here, anyway."

Piney grunted. "You're to be an invalid for a day or so. Lucky too. That Molly makes a sweet nurse, I bet!"

Rick flushed. "I don't need a nurse, Piney! What I need is some information. How did those fires begin? I reported observations on that last jump and everybody seemed to clam up. Don't tell me a succession of fires like these in this area is 'just one of those things'!"

Piney's eyes were cold and shrewd in the reflected firelight. "They're beginnin' to listen to what you been sayin'," he said. "No. They weren't just chance, I know that." He hesitated. "Rick, those stories about your father . . ."

Rick sat up.

Piney pressed him back gently. "Maybe those 'prospectors' did find the treasure, after all," he said softly. "But where does that leave us?"

"I don't think they've found it yet. But" —Rick's eyes clouded—" the Fund must be here somewhere—or somebody thinks it's here—and that somebody's getting careless searching for it!" He took a deep breath.

Piney let silence come down before he

said gently, "It's something to think about, Rick." He got up. Molly was coming towards them, her trim figure outlined by the crimson play of refracted flames from the numerous small fires in the clearing. "Yeah, something to think on, Rick, boy. Me and the sheriff have done some thinkin'. I expect some others have, too. See yuh!"

He moved off as Molly came up. She crouched beside Rick, opening a small case she was carrying. He watched her when she gave him a shy smile, watched while the firelight played over her capable hands, marvelling at the whiteness of them and their quiet strength. He hardly felt the unguents, nor the pain as she applied bandages to his shoulder and wrist, which had been burned badly.

"Don't worry," she said gently. "You won't be laid up long, Rick. You're to be ferried back and then you'll probably be under observation until sometime tomorrow. Brad Hovey too." She searched his face. "I've just talked with Brad. He's

—puzzled. You risked your life and almost lost your own when you pulled him out, Rick. They're all surprised at your being able to do it at all! It didn't need an eye-witness to tell what a job you did ; the signs were plain. It was a brave thing."

Rick shook his head. " Part of my job," he said. " Hovey's a smoke jumper ; so am I. That's all. The rest doesn't count."

" Maybe," she said slowly. Then, as she picked up her things, " But it counts with me, Rick. See you back at the Base! "

Rick's eyes followed her as she moved away. Quiet, efficient, lovely. The kind of girl . . . Rick let his eyes close. He hadn't known it but he had been given a sedative and his muscles relaxed into sleep. There was no longer any pain.

CHAPTER ELEVEN

THE FIRE RING

RICK woke in the dispensary-hospital at the Pinnacle Base.

Along about noon after he had been under examination by a series of doctors, Molly came. And with her, bounding into the place as if nothing had happened, but obviously overjoyed at a reunion with his master, was Smoky. Smoky leaped on to the bed and started to lick Rick's face, but Molly laughed and pulled him away.

After Molly had gone, there were two more consulting physicians. They bent over Rick and talked across his nude body, just as though he were not there. Scientific terms, medical jargon. He heard their words, but they meant little to him. When the doctors were finished with him and were drawing up the sheets, he looked up and said :

" I'm not bad enough off to be in bed! "

The elder of the two laughed. " And we're so blamed short of smoke jumpers around here that you're not going to stay in bed! To-day and a good night's sleep and you report for limited duty, as usual, to-morrow morning. Now go to sleep— *you will*! "

Rick soon found what they meant by that. On the following day, late in the afternoon, after a last check up, Rick was released for duty. " Light duty " was specified, but Whelan laughed when he heard that, back at the barracks.

" You know what happened just before you got back in here, Rick? " he said. " They called me on the telephone from district headquarters. The chief! Guess what he had to say! "

Rick looked ready to be amused. He stared across the room. There was Hovey, partly in shadow, and there was Smoky. Hovey thought he wasn't being seen as he carefully pulled a wadded paper from his shirt and unwrapped it. Rick watched. Smoky had been on his way to other amusements, but what was in Brad Hovey's hand held him.

It was a bone, a big meaty bone!

Rick had to grin in spite of himself. Hovey didn't want it known that he had a strong liking for the pooch; he feared " riding " on account of his jealousy of Rick. Yet underneath he loved dogs—and this one especially!

Rick thought, He might as well like Smoky! If it hadn't been for Smoky, I'd never have known he was there last night. I saved him? Put it that Smoky and I combined did!

Whelan's rasping voice was going on: " Asked me if we needed some help out here! That's what! Didn't we have enough jumpers to hold down this area? And if we did, why was there a new blaze starting up every night? Said the ground Rangers were on the job, checking. They'd spotted what incipient fires there were . . ." Whelan paused, smiling that crooked smile of his. " 'Incipient,' in case you heroes missed it in school, means fires likely to start, areas ready to break out. And the regular Rangers say they've covered them all and reported 'em. And in spite of that, now it seems like we're jumpin' every ten minutes. How do you like that? "

There was silence. His listeners waited for more. But there was no more. Whelan had made his point.

"We all took that work, of course," some-one said. " But it fails to take into account one thing : ' incipient fire ' or not—and they told us what the word means, Chief!—you can check all you like and still if a fire is deliberately started, your check's not worth a hoot! Even if you've been over the ground a dozen times! "

Whelan nodded gravely. Across the room Smoky was licking his chops. Hovey was staring down at him.

" It's getting plenty hot here," a jumper put in. " And now we get called sissies for not knowing in advance. I went in for re-forestation and I think maybe I'll apply to go back to it. They don't ride you when your trees don't grow in time, anyway! "

" You'll be back here," another jeered. " You've had your taste of smoke, son, and you won't be able to get away from it for long! "

There was no denial of that, even from the first speaker who had threatened to "desert."

None of the jumpers had mentioned the

narrow escape Hovey and Rick had had the night before. But there was no sign of friendliness between the two ; they had scarcely spoken to each other since. Once Hovey had ventured :

" They told me what you did, Rick. I don't suppose I need to say I appreciate it. You—you didn't have to pull me out, you know . . . and I know it too."

" I did have to, if I was following the rules, Hovey. Let's let it ride that way, shall we ? "

Rick thought of that exchange and then looked back at Hovey. Whelan was in the doorway, scowling. It was about time for the men to begin drifting off to the Coke Palace. Some had already gone. The night was balmy, pleasant. But even here there came the penetrating taint of wood smoke as from a distant conflagration, breeze-borne over miles of forest. It was always there, a constant reminder.

Into the musing silence, the sound broke. Feet came pounding. Whelan's voice—he'd never get to drink *that* pop, Rick thought! The siren blasted the air into shreds and on the heels of its first wild shriek a motor coughed and roared to life.

In the doorway Whelan stopped only long enough to bark : " All crews out! That's an alert! Snap it up! "

They needed no spur. Most of them needed a rest, but they were ready just the same.

Then the barracks speaker was turned on and Whelan's voice was barking over the intercom from his end of the room, attacking every ear.

" We're checking all equipment—everybody!—before anybody leaves here! "

Whelan himself, with the habitual ease of his long service, was the first to have his equipment checked and he was at the doorway, his paraphernalia alongside him, a full two minutes before the first of his crew got to him.

He looked like a man from Mars.

So did the rest when they were in their

gear. Rick saw Hovey go up to check, saw Whelan's nod, marvelled at the coolness of his chief. Whelan might bark and rant, but when emergency came he was as cool as ice. He didn't look the least bit hurried now, but no single movement was wasted. Rick thought that perhaps by this time even Whelan might have begun to have his doubts as to the innocence of these continuous alarms.

Then he was in front of his chief, being inspected. Whelan tugged at his harness, examined his extinguisher thrower, checked to see that it was fully loaded, patted him on the shoulder with a laconic :

" Thought you'd talked yourself into a rest, eh? You should know better by now, Rick, boy. Okay, get along! "

Rick tumbled out, found the searching beam and went as fast as he could towards the waiting plane. His equipment weighed a lot. He moved the way he imagined a diver might at the bottom of the ocean. He might try to move fast but his equipment impeded him ; it dragged heavily at legs and arms and shoulders.

Hovey was ahead of him into the plane. Hovey had not been spared either. He wore a bandage on his forehead but it fitted snugly under the rim of his helmet.

Rick tumbled down the steps into the plane, at the heels of Ladd Malcolm. He turned just before he dropped down and saw Molly, watching. His pulses gave a leap. Something told him she had been waiting for him to turn ; her arms high above her head, she was waving to him with a clasped-hands gesture that meant good luck!

Rick waved back, smiling, and hurried into his place, rolling against Malcolm as he found the bucket seat.

She'd been waiting there, not to tell the others good-bye, but to wave to him. Rick hugged the thought to himself. It made him feel warm inside.

The roar of the giant motors drowned out sound completely. Even the intercom was dead now. Whelan made gestures. The engines continued to rev up; the ship wobbled against her chocks, straining to go. The floodlights made daylight of the tarmac. Long pencil beams from the fuselage stabbed upwards into the night sky, clear and deeply blue.

The big doors slammed. Sound inside came louder with the cutting off of outside sound. It was bedlam. Then the ship began to move, taxying slowly, gathering speed. It went roaring down the long runway, lifted a little, settled as if to make sure, lifted again—then its wheels left the ground and once more the smoke-jumper crew of Pinnacle Base was airborne.

In spite of the weight of the big plane, they gained altitude rapidly. The plane pointed almost at once up into the clouds and made a spiralling circuit of the field from a height of not more than three thousand feet before the pilot levelled off and pointed north and westward.

There was talking aboard the ship but

scarcely anyone could hear what was said. The voices were drowned out. There was something oddly angry—a sense, Rick felt, of resentment in the engines' roar as they bore the giant transport out and up through the blue-black night. Resentment at over-work! He laughed at himself for the fancy.

Below, the great expanse of forests stretched to the farthest horizon. Here and there the unbroken velvet of them was pierced by stray clusters of lights, marking small towns and hamlets with lives of their own, far from the fire menace. Sleeping villages, places that might be no more than a post office, still awake but serene.

The tree-tops made a velvet pattern of bluish-black, oddly like a tumbled flat blanket. And through and among them, forgotten forest trails or old roads wound, used by loggers or by hunters in season but otherwise lost. These were no more than thin traceries that might have been lighter lines engraved on a great map.

A half-hour after the take-off—and some of that time had been spent in circling—they came within sight of the new blaze. The smoke jumpers crowded to the bays to observe what lay below.

A forest fire by night can be an awesome picture. This fire was in the same spot where Rick had jumped on that first occasion, when he had found Piney—again. But by night the scene was frighteningly different.

The slopes of the lofty mountain dropped down into the spot. The slopes, though thickly forested, were still unharmed. Through the cloak of trees and verdure covering them silver streams came meandering down towards the confluence where they met larger streams. These streams made threads in the entire pattern.

The fire, this time . . . Rick caught his breath!

He could see it plainly enough, he assured himself grimly. He was coming back to where he had started from : the spot that embraced the cabin at stream's edge—the place where his father had been last reported alive!

The forested area where so much talk had been given to a vein of mercury some years before. That was legend and a joke now—unless the searchers had found something new—but what was of importance was that this was the spot to which his father had been traced, the place that had swallowed him up on that long-ago night!

It was fully ablaze now. There was a ring of flame that could not have been " flash fire." It was too well patterned ; they could all see that.

It was like a great coiled snake made of shining rubies, its heart blackened but its ring flaming. At the stream's edge, the old tower still stood, visible even from the air with its continual spilling of its burden of excess water.

There must be considerable wind down below because the bent of the flames was definitely towards the south.

But no sign of anything human, at least not yet.

The plane banked wide, coming down gradually. It made a new probing circle over the area, its own roar hitting back to the ears of its occupants as its exhaust caught up with it. It was a deafening sound.

Malcolm was at Rick's side.

" Same place you found your old pal, isn't it? " he shouted.

Rick nodded. He searched for Piney's cabin, but couldn't locate it among the trees. The flames had not yet lighted that section but they were eating towards it hungrily.

Once again they swooped. Whelan's voice came over the intercom :

" Crews to stations! Ready! Number One Crew! "

Rick stepped up, along with Malcolm this time.

Whelan went grimly about his business of checking equipment. The light in the big interior was dim yellow but good enough for him.

Each man took his turn. Whelan was a hard taskmaster. Rough and comradely on the ground, on his job he acknowledged no friends. They were all machines trained for a job, and his job was to see that the machines worked smoothly. When Rick came up, he had a grin for him.

" If you still got that headache, this is the stuff to get rid of it for you. You're okay! Next! "

CHAPTER TWELVE

THE MYSTERY IS SOLVED

RICK failed to take note of the order of
their dropping. His head throbbed; but
his body was eager. He did not see Malcolm
tumble overside, the figures in between;

then his own number came up as Whelan
stood there roaring his commands, every
inch of him a machine now.

A moment later he was in space again,
fingers closed tightly on his harness ring,
counting. His eyes opened against his will
and he saw, just as his 'chute caught a full
hand of breeze and held it, what lay below.

Rick swayed there, pulling at the cords
to direct his descent towards the fire's
centre.

What he saw confirmed the impression he
had had from the air. The fire ringed the
familiar area where Piney's cabin stood. Just
below the cabin, there was the silver trickle
of the stream that fed into the larger stream,
and from which the logs had, in other days,
been floated down into the river below.

So great had been the fire's headway that
its red glow lighted up a great deal of the
map below.

Thus Rick was able to survey from the
slowing of his descent what otherwise he
might not have been able to observe. The

fire had been begun with a purpose, and that purpose was to draw off investigation from its instigators. There was too much of a pattern in it for it to be set down as a natural blaze ; the fire ring cut off most of the area below to where the cabin-storehouse at the water's edge stood alone. The fire ring was a defence against invasion from the ground right up to that point—but it was not safe from invasion from the air!

Yes, that was the pattern. And Rick was coming to understand at last what the pattern meant.

His boot tops touched a branch ; he had dropped lower than he had been able to judge from the night sky. He jerked his cords, felt a breeze take and lift him slightly until he was passing through an area where only his helmet saved him from asphyxiation from the billowing clouds of smoke.

His helmet and goggles were a protection but even they could not lend him vision. He had to use his own judgment.

He must judge when he was close enough

to the ground to release his 'chute. He tried to estimate his height, but the clouds of smoke were too dense. Then, when the silk above him caught again and started a real tear, he let go.

When he fell it was to drop about seven feet. He landed easily, cutting himself free and freeing his equipment in the same single motion.

For only an instant he stood there, working his limbs free for the task ahead. Then, remembering the direction of the fire's core, and familiar with the terrain, he started towards it.

There was no time or reason for breaking fire lanes or attempting to isolate separate blazes. There were too many separate blazes and yet they were all part of the one blaze.

Smoke clouds came roaring towards him out of bush that one moment was standing free and proud and the next went up in quick " flash " blazes. But he fought his way doggedly towards the core, understanding that to begin the fight at this point would be futile.

Once he had battled his way into the centre of the fire ring, he brought his " thrower " into action. With it fanning out a splayed hose in front of him, he fought his way to the opposite side of the ring. There he halted, shaking his head and trying to clear his vision.

He could make out the water's edge and the storehouse, the platform of which jutted out over the water. A smoke cloud rolled across his vision but in that instant he had been certain that he saw figures—and not the goggled, cloaked figures of smoke jumpers.

He worked his way towards the water tower. He remembered it well. If some of the precious fluid up there could be released, it would form a dampening spray. Often in the past, its liberal spraying had been put to use in times of drought. But if enemies were here, they would know that too.

There were moments when even his goggles were of no aid. Of course he could have simply gone ahead with extinguisher tank and fought what was in front of him. But Rick knew that that was not the answer to this problem.

He stopped, reeled back, lost in a white fog of thick smoke. He couldn't even see his own gloved hands. But he had retained his sense of direction.

He stood on sloping ground and he knew that ground well enough to gauge where he must be now. About twenty yards below him, he judged, was the storage house, near where his father's body had been found. And beyond that the small stream. To the right of him, at an angle, the water tower lifted. Someone must have thought of that. Even as he stood there orienting himself, he was aware of a fine spray like mist drizzling past his goggles. It streaked their surfaces.

He found his breath coming hard in spite of the oxygen tank he carried. The air he was getting was mixed with something that had a taint in it.

The goggles framed a scene like something on a TV screen. Bushes were there one minute, juniper and scrub pine and stunted oak; then they became a puff of flame and were erased as though they had never been.

Animals came scuttling past; he noticed them for the first time. Rabbits and foxes, scurrying for air. Some bear cubs. A deer and a doe and three fawns, backing and filling behind four lost vixens, all of them terrified. Looking blindly for some lane of escape.

They headed by instinct towards the water.

Rick aroused himself. He decided to cut a way through in front of himself and try to gain the water tower.

His heavy boots seemed to weigh tons. Every movement became slow-motion.

Then the smoke gave a great puff and whirled away from his path, in a side current of air that only served to fan it farther on, and he had a moment's clear view of the tower, the sloping terrain, and the storage shack by the water edge. Something else, too, that instantly cleared away the fog from his eyes and alerted him.

There were figures ahead. He saw Brad Hovey, recognising him from that queer swastika pattern on his suit. He, too, must have thought of the water tower.

At that instant Hovey was trapped by two men, trapped with his back to the storage shack above the stream. Ventner and Cadre! —the two strangers Rick had seen in town that day—the " mercury prospectors."

Hovey was backing away, but they were coming at him. From somewhere they had procured old asbestos suits but their faces were protected only by heavy cloths that had been soaked, evidently, in water. Their feet were protected by heavy logging boots.

They were closing in on Hovey.

Brad was waving his extinguisher at them, backing.

Rick forced himself into action. Clogged as his body was with the thick smoke that had somehow managed to seep through his armour, he moved slowly ; he realised that himself. But he moved.

Sometimes he lost sight of his objective. But they hadn't yet seen him, he knew—he was approaching the scene at an angle and smoke obscured him too.

The ground shelved towards the three figures. Hovey caught sight of him first, he thought, but he couldn't be sure. Something in the way Hovey gave a start told him.

Then, just as he was closing in, he stumbled. The roar of the holocaust all about them deafened Hovey's attackers to his approach as well as to his fall. He landed and rolled, and when he jerked up he was directly behind them. He could hear, from Ventner's thick lips, lips puffed with heat and scorch :

" You got in our way, smoke jumper, and that's all. We don't happen to want that water tank in action—it'll bring people around here too fast. What we do want is just behind you—and you're in our way. Get the idea? "

Hovey half-turned to glance over his shoulder. All he could see was the storage shack at the edge of the stream. One of the big men laughed harshly.

" Yeah, you got it in one! " He coughed ; the smoke was getting at last to his bull-like lungs. "Yeah—in one! " he repeated. "Ain't you been shootin' off your mouth about Harding and that lost loot? Been hearin' a lot of your lip. Well, now you're goin' to find you was on the right track—only you're not going to be able to go back and prove it! Because that loot you talked so much about—that loot's just behind you! "

Rick raised his head, shaking it to clear it of fumes. He needed to hear more. He did.

" That night something scared old Harding and he lit out with the loot. Maybe he knew we was shadowin' him right along. He lit out to hide it. He did, curse him, before we caught up with him in the dark. He hid it——"

" Then you "—Hovey's voice came harsh and torn through his mask—" you're the ones that killed him! You killed Rick Harding's father. You're the highjackers! "

The bullish laugh came again. " In one, repeat! "

" Only," Ventner's companion broke in, the same rasp in his thick voice, " we didn't do our highjackin' fast enough. Harding suspected we were on his track and he got out with the treasure and managed to hide it. He wouldn't talk when we finally caught up with him and so he had to get the works! We couldn't afford to have him talkin' after- wards—we were too well known in these parts. Oh, yes, we were known! But a whale of a lot younger then, and we've changed a lot. Even Piney Lane didn't recognise us, at least he wasn't sure. And Ventner's beard helped too. Anyway, we knew the loot was hid, and we waited. Now—now we know where he stashed it! "

" Then it was the loot you were after all the time! " Hovey gasped. " *You* started those fires! "

" Some of 'em. We got careless. Some places we wanted to draw inquisitive noses away from this particular part. We didn't count on the smoke jumpers being called in. They're too nosy for us. But when you guys did get here we had to keep on with the fires business, to draw you away from our target and make you think there were just a lot of fires anyway and it wasn't just here! "

Hovey's laugh, when it came, was oddly harsh. " And do you know what you proved to-night? Unless the smoke jumpers get to you, you're due to wind up cremated in this blaze. You and your stolen loot, along with the rest! You can't work your way out, not without help from us! "

For an instant that seemed to sober the

two ruffians. They turned to look at each other questioningly. Then—it was big Jeff Cadre whose snarl came :

" What's it matter? You know us now, and you can't talk. That loot's in the storage shack behind you. Harding took it in there and stashed it. We found out from somebody who talked too much one night in town ; he didn't know what he was saying, and didn't know we could take bearings from it . . . Harding had been digging for weeks, knowing somebody was on his tracks. The loot's under the flooring where the door-sill opens on to the landing platform over the water. The water hides it! We know that now. And now you know it. We're going to take care of you first and then take our own chances getting out. We didn't come this far—risk this much— for nothing! "

They were moving in on the helpless Brad Hovey. Rick came to his knees, to his feet. He could see Brad raising his extinguisher in a helpless gesture. Yet that fluid could be dangerous to a man unprotected—and be-sides, it was all Brad had to fight with!

Rick threw himself towards the confusion that swept the smoke-filled hollow. His head was clearing at last; the closeness to the ground had done that. The less poisoned air there had supplemented the oxygen in his tank. He knew the smoke must be getting to the two thugs too, strong as they looked.

Just at that instant a flash fire caught at a new patch of brush and sprang into lurid flame. Rick charged through that flame as the two men half-turned, scared, and his extinguisher fluid bored straight into their faces.

Hovey gave a cry and went to work.

Ventner charged broad-shouldered and hard at Rick. Rick met him head-on with a hose of fluid. He reeled back.

Rick charged downslope. He loosed the small axe from his belt equipment, and through the smoke haze saw a pistol levelled at him. He threw the axe then—and charged.

The pistol seemed to blaze almost in his face. He could hear voices somewhere behind him but they were confused.

Ventner was on him now, pounds heavier, unencumbered by the heavy clothing which was protection against flame but just the opposite in personal combat.

The pistol exploded again. Rick felt something burn his shoulder. He closed with Ventner. He could no longer see Hovey, but he heard a second pistol explode.

Then he was down and Ventner's big hands were clawing at his throat.

Rick fought back fiercely. He and his antagonist rolled over and over, down towards the water's edge. The pistol had become lost in the fury.

Smoke poured like a pall over the scene.

From somewhere, part of the same nightmare, no doubt, there came to Rick's ears Piney's high-pitched voice. Then other voices. . . .

Hovey gave a shout, hurled off his antagonist by some miracle, and began to run. The blazing ring of flame was close to all of them by now. The clothing of the two malefactors was on fire in several patches.

Cadre turned. Even with his great strength, it was plain to be seen that the thick, poisonous smoke was getting to him. He set out after Brad Hovey, but his movements were slow, laboured.

Rick continued to fight back, knowing now it was life or death. He struck blindly. What was Hovey up to? He had headed for the water tower.

But Ventner had a dogged strength. He found Rick's throat with his big hairy-backed hands and his fingers closed.

Rick turned, twisted ; his free hand found the nozzle of his extinguisher. It worked around. He pressed. A stream of acid fluid streaked out. How he had located the tank was a mystery to him even then ; it must have become unfastened during the struggle. But its nozzle was there!

The nozzle sprayed—straight upward into

those red pin-pointed eyes and the cruel mouth.

Ventner reeled back, blinded. Hovey was crying out from somewhere behind the swirling smoke.

Rick got to his feet, the nozzle still in his hand. He groped for the axe handle. But just then the smoke reached him, too, and his swaying developed into a collapse.

Suddenly, without warning, the water tower began to speak in its own language. Hovey had gained it and released its spray.

The rain came pelting down among the trees. And at the same time those distant voices became real. It hadn't been his imagination! He had really heard Piney's voice.

Then it was Piney's and Whelan's mingled, and no longer a question of voices but of figures breaking through a ring of flame and smoke. Rick swung once again, hard, at Ventner, and felt the man go sagging to his knees.

He made a leap. His hands fastened about

Ventner's throat as they came up—Piney leading the way. Behind Piney came Whelan and Malcolm and the crew. They gave a roar and closed in.

Another roar was in Rick's head too. His eyes closed and he sank back. He was still clutching Ventner's throat when they got there.

The rest Rick didn't know for quite a time. But he knew Smoky was there, and the voices he knew were real enough, this time. Then he let himself fade into a cloud of his own making that was not part of the smoke clouds but of his own brain.

Brad Hovey and Rick Harding lay in beds side by side at the Base Hospital. It was full daylight the day following the fire. Both jumpers had slept until noon.

Rick raised a slightly burned hand to his head to find the hand bandaged, and then he discovered there was a bandage coming down partly over his left eye. His left forearm was bandaged too. There was something tightly drawn around his ribs and he realised he must have been hit by a bullet and was probably taped up.

Otherwise, he felt all right—there was no pain. And when he looked across to the next cot he saw Brad Hovey lying there. Hovey had been waiting to catch his gaze and he was smiling a wistful, somehow shy, smile.

Rick smiled back, and said, " We bought ourselves some trouble last night, I guess."

" Yeah," Hovey returned. " But they tell me we did okay. I've been awake an hour or more. You all right now? "

" If they'll lay off that siren for forty-eight hours! " Rick grinned.

" No danger of that," Hovey told him. " We ended the epidemic last night. They've got those two men in jail. Ventner and Cadre. Hospital ward of the jail—in the big town. Claim both of them are wanted for almost everything under the sun. I heard your friend the sheriff talking. Seems Piney Lane forced him to send for fingerprints and ask Washington for ' flyers ' covering their activities ; the F.B.I. came in. They found out plenty, stretching back for years."

" It began," Rick mused, " years and years ago. But maybe this job at Pinnacle was their first one and there might have been time in between when they weren't playing crooked. Anyway . . ." He closed his eyes.

So his hunch and Piney's agreement had both been proved right.

Later Piney told him all about it, sitting beside the hospital bed.

" Not that those two started all the fires in these parts, not by a jugful! It started with fires begun by accident or carelessness while they were looking around ; that gave them ideas and they saw their chance when there were real fires.

" They built more of them at odd spots to keep you boys busy--also to keep the Federal men engaged in thinking of incendiaries instead of thinking of wanted criminals comin' back to cash in on their crimes. It was a good notion they had, dependin' on where you sit. But it wound up by trappin' the very ones who dreamed it up. Neither of them will ever see the outside of a jail again. They . . ." Piney hesitated.

Brad Hovey was leaning over to catch every word.

Rick said, " And they killed my father, didn't they? "

" They won't admit it—yet. But it's plain enough they did. They'll break down before long, no doubt about that. Cadre's almost ready to talk now and they've placed 'em apart so when he breaks he won't be afraid of his partner in crime." Piney added, " They always do ' sing,' those birds, when the goin' gets tough! "

" What's the rest of it, Piney? "

The old woodsman's face cracked in a big smile.

" The best," he said. " The story's out now, at last. Your father went into that cabin and hid the loot; I told you he'd known somebody was on his track. They had to kill him when they caught him comin' back and he wouldn't talk. But still they didn't know where he'd cached the treasure. That Fund—yes, Sheriff Lincoln and his boys found it this morning." He nodded towards Brad Hovey. "That was after your pal here told us what he'd heard them say. He didn't know all, but he knew enough so we could go to work, knowin' where to look. Yep, we found it. . . ." Piney chuckled. "All of it!"

Rick let his eyes close. He was vindicated. What was more, his father's name had been cleared. He could face the world with no stain on his name. And Brad Hovey had helped.

He understood now the meaning of that wistful little smile on Hovey's face, a smile appealing for forgiveness. He put out his hand to stretch between the two cots.

"Thanks, pal," he said.

Hovey was embarrassed. "Maybe," he grinned shamefacedly, "maybe you're not sorry you pulled me out that time, heh?

But we both came through and that's what counts."

There was that, and—a little later—Molly and Smoky. Smoky looked chagrined at having missed the final act. But he was happy between the two men to whom he had given his affection, and he did not hesitate to show it.

The big bulk of Whelan behind her, Molly sat in a chair between the two cots. She held Rick's good hand and her eyes shone.

"No need for me to tell you I'm glad, Rick," she whispered. "You know it, I guess." She looked at Hovey and smiled. "Glad for a lot of things," she said, "all at once. For you two, for example. Even if the going was tough up to here!"

"Smoke jumping," Whelan opined, "is supposed to be tough. All its angles. I guess you boys found that out."

Brad Hovey lay back with his eyes closed; he was not asleep, but he looked happier. He murmured, "Rick, ask 'Simon Legree'

Whelan do we need to take another jump before to-morrow. Tell him I'm plenty tired right now. And—" his voice broke a little as his free hand came down and found Smoky's rough head, nuzzled the lifted ears —" and happy."

Molly smiled across Rick towards him. Her eyes were misty. " It looks," she said, " as though everybody's happy, at last! "

Rick smiled too, looking at her, feeling her warm hand in his. " I know I am," he said quietly.

The End